ORPHANS of ST HALIBUT'S

⚒ PAMELA'S REVENGE ⚒

Praise for *The Orphans of St Halibut's*:

'Stupendous and hilarious. Deliciously disgusting . . . and filled to the brim with dark humour. Perfect for fans of Lemony Snicket.' Hana Tooke, author of *The Unadoptables*

'Dark, funny and very, very clever. With gloriously gothic artwork from David Tazzyman' Rashmi Sideshpande, author of *Dosh* and *Good News*

'Funny, dark, eccentric and clever' Nicola Penfold, author of *Where the World Turns Wild*

'A fabulously funny tale of clever orphans, rambling houses, angry goats and grizzly ends' Kirsty Applebaum, author of *The Middler*

'This book will make you snort, squirm and scream with laughter!' Dashe Roberts, author of *Sticky Pines: The Bigwoof Conspiracy*

'A wonderful caper' Marina Hyde, *Guardian* columnist

'A brilliant bunch of characters. David Tazzyman's illustrations are spot on' MyBookCorner Blog

Also by Sophie Wills

The Orphans of St Halibut's

Illustrated by David Tazzyman

The ORPHANS of ST HALIBUT'S

⚔ PAMELA'S REVENGE ⚔

Sophie Wills

MACMILLAN CHILDREN'S BOOKS

First published 2021 by Macmillan Children's Books
an imprint of Pan Macmillan
The Smithson, 6 Briset Street, London EC1M 5NR
EU representative: Macmillan Publishers Ireland Ltd, 1st Floor,
The Liffey Trust Centre, 117–126 Sheriff Street Upper
Dublin 1, D01 YC43
Associated companies throughout the world
www.panmacmillan.com

ISBN 978-1-5290-1339-9

1 3 5 7 9 8 6 4 2

A CIP catalogue record for this book is available from the British Library.

Printed and bound by CPI Group (UK) Ltd, Croydon CR0 4YY

First published 2021 by Macmillan Children's Books
an imprint of Pan Macmillan
The Smithson, 6 Briset Street, London EC1M 5NR
EU representative: Macmillan Publishers Ireland Ltd, 1st Floor,
The Liffey Trust Centre, 117–126 Sheriff Street Upper, Dublin 1

For Rob, Fraser, and Cameron

✌ Chapter One ✌

'**T**he whole point of Miss Happyday being dead,' said Herc, 'is that we don't have to do this sort of thing anymore.'

His sister's grip did not slacken as she dragged him down the steep hill away from St Halibut's Home for Waifs and Strays. Sometimes Herc felt she could be a lot like their not-so-dear departed matron, especially when it came to stopping him from doing what he wanted.

Herc's latest marshmallow recipe had produced a fantastically glossy, thick, pale liquid and turned the kitchen air into breathable treacle; the ultimate sweet, fluffy treat was now cooling on the counter. He'd only just managed to pour it out before Tig had stormed into the kitchen yelling that they were going to be late, that all the other orphans were down at the festival already, and if he didn't come right NOW there would be consequences. She didn't say what *kind* of consequences, but over the eight long years of his life he had learned that if you were promised them, they were never good.

Marshmallows were Herc's latest cookery obsession. The quest to find the perfect recipe had been consuming his every waking thought for weeks. It was particularly unfair that he had been forced to abandon them to go to the Sad Sack Festival, an event so dangerously dull that it had actually killed one of Arfur's pigeons the previous year.

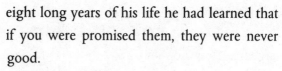

'I'm worried, Tig. Remember what happened to Fevvers.'

Tig continued to stride onwards, her fingers coiled around his hand. 'Herc, the festival did not kill Fevvers – that's stupid. Birds don't live very long. It was his time, that's all.'

'If you're going to die of old age you do it in your nest, while you're asleep. You don't suddenly drop out of the sky and into the tombola.'

Tig's jaw clenched. 'Look. I don't care what Arfur told you, Fevvers did not die of boredom.' Their con-man friend *may* have helped save their lives a few months earlier and *was* still loyally keeping the secret that they were living all alone up at St Halibut's, but he was also in

2

the habit of winding them up. 'Arfur says a lot of things. If you believe half of them you're even less brainy than his pigeons. Now stop moaning and try to have fun.'

As they walked on to Sad Sack High Street, it quickly became clear that fun was going to be in short supply.

Bickley Brimstone, owner of the pharmacy and President of the Sad Sack Business Association, organized the festival every year, though it wasn't clear exactly what there was to celebrate about the town's miserable existence. Mainly, the event seemed to be about forcing everyone to spend more money in his shop.

Bickley got very offended if the townsfolk didn't attend the festival. If you stayed away, for the other 364 days of the year he would give you the wrong change, accidentally shut doors in your face and drop heavy things on your foot.

It was for this reason that Tig had insisted all the orphans at St Halibut's should attend. The last thing they wanted was Bickley taking a hostile interest in them. The people of Sad Sack hadn't noticed – or if they had, they didn't care – that the matron of St Halibut's, Miss Happyday, had not been seen for months. She'd never exactly been popular, but that didn't mean the orphans could be careless. They'd already had one narrow escape. DEATH – the Department for Education, Assimilation,

Training and Health – might look the other way if they heard rumours about St Halibut's, but if someone like Bickley Brimstone discovered the truth and shoved it in their faces, DEATH would probably feel obliged to do something about it.

'This is the worst festival in the whole world.' Herc kicked a stone at the *Welcome to Sad Sack* sign propped up against a bin, and it fell face down in the dirt.

Tig didn't disagree. It was one of those events that looked a lot better on the flyer than it did in reality. The promised 'Fun Pool' was one of the bigger potholes on the high street, filled with dirty water; the 'Helter Skelter' was run by a sullen teenager who took a penny off you and then gave you a shove down the spiral iron staircase outside the Mending House.

DEATH still sent wayward children to the Mending House for punishment and re-education, but since Maisie had taken over from the dastardly Ainderby Myers, life inside had changed somewhat. Under Myers' rule, Mended children had woven and spun cotton until their fingers bled, but Maisie had her new recruits sitting around a cosy fire on beanbags, chatting, laughing and knitting. She refused to call them Mended, except on the paperwork; to her they were the Poppets. She sold whatever they produced and used the money to care for them as best she could,

4

which was a *lot*: every night, she tucked each Poppet into bed and read a bedtime story while they sipped hot cocoa. It was all very nice, but the St Halibut's orphans preferred their freedom.

And Herc really had no right to moan. True, the first weeks after the matron's death had been tricky: Tig, Herc and their friend Stef had come close to losing St Halibut's and·spending the rest of their lives in the Mending House. Its Guvnor, Ainderby Myers, had threatened their very lives. But Herc had accidentally blown a huge hole in the side of the Mending House and they'd escaped. Bizarrely, this had resulted in Tig banning him from playing with any more substances from the pharmacy, rather than recognizing his clearly exceptional chemistry skills.

Still, all the poor Mended children had been rescued and Myers hadn't been seen since. For the first few weeks they had all lived together at St Halibut's, a riotous crowd of around forty children who could make the windows rattle with their noisy games. But Arfur had pointed out that, unlike the St Halibut's children, most of the Mended were not orphans, and he had insisted on tracing their families.

One by one, he had returned them to their joyful and surprised parents in every corner of Garbashire, saying simply that they had completed their sentences at the Mending House. There was no mention of explosions, or rescues, and the Mended children themselves were sworn to silence.

It was the right thing to do, Herc supposed. But all the same, he missed them – especially because now he was back to being the youngest. Just six of them remained: him and Tig, of course, plus their friend Stef, then Nellie and Cuthbert, the two St Cod's orphans they had picked up along the way, and finally Ashna, the Mended burglar

who was also an orphan. They were only four or five years older than him, but the way they acted sometimes, they might as well be his grandparents.

The day dragged on and on. Each shop had a stall outside it, decorated with miserably faded bunting, as well as their usual wares inside. Herc searched for Ma Yeasty's stall, which would be the only one with something entertaining

going on (and, of course, a snack or two to eat).

He found her bakery stand being manned by Arty Chokes, the greengrocer. Arty was busy removing sweet treats from the display and replacing them with what, from a distance, looked excitingly like severed heads, but on closer inspection were revealed to be rows of wilted cauliflowers covered with mould spots.

'Where's Ma Yeasty?' Herc asked, unable to hide his disappointment.

Arty frowned at him. 'Gone for a lie-down. Just as well, if you ask me. Look at this – doughnuts! Disgusting. You can even *see* the sugar on them – she tried to tell me they were just dusty. Must think I was born yesterday. That woman has a blatant disregard for the health of our citizens.'

Herc gazed at the doughnut-filled bin, his mouth watering. 'Oh.'

Ma Yeasty had told him about her plan for the stall: she was going to run a 'Guess the Weight of the Cake' competition and have a hoopla, with doughnuts to throw instead of wooden rings. You could eat any that landed accurately on the pegs. And, knowing Ma Yeasty, any that didn't as well. It was the only thing about the festival he'd been looking forward to.

He spent the next hour wandering sulkily through

the streets as the summer sun dimmed gradually, every now and then checking his pulse in case he was, in fact, breathing his last and going the same way as Fevvers. He waved at Sue Perglue as she sat wretchedly at her hardware stall, advertising a contest to win a small packet of sandpaper. Unsurprisingly, few people had taken her up on the offer.

Maisie, the much kinder replacement Guvnor of the Mending House, was proudly showing off all the knitted items the new young residents had made – scarves and gloves were festooned across her stall in a riot of bright colours.

'How're you getting on with that hat, young man?' Maisie called to Herc as he passed.

'Oh, fine, thanks,' he called back, and walked a little faster. Since Pamela, their angry pet goat, had eaten most of their cash, the orphans had started to earn money by knitting for Maisie. It might be early summer, but in her view, knitted products were suitable all year round. After a few lessons, some had taken to it more than others. Cuthbert had produced a number of chic cardigans using advanced stitches he'd looked up in the Crafts section of Arfur's mobile library; Ashna had managed a single, wonky scarf; Stef had accidentally stabbed himself in the stomach with a knitting needle while making a blanket that consisted mainly of a large hole; and Herc's bobble hat had never made it past the bobble stage.

Bickley Brimstone's pharmacy had a queue of people around it and Herc spotted Nellie watching from a short distance.

'He's still doing that swindle with the tea,' she told him, sounding both disgusted and admiring at the same time. Bickley Brimstone had been trying to sell a load of some mysterious herbal tea for weeks now. To start with, no one had bought it. So he had begun claiming not only that the tea would cure any sickness, indeed any problem, but that he could tell people's fortunes once they'd drunk it, all for just a shilling. This seemed to be working much better as a sales tactic.

Nellie shook her head at the queuers. 'I'll tell yer fortunes, ya wallies! You're gonna get a lot poorer. There ya go, that'll be a shilling, mate.' She held out her palm to the nearest man, who obligingly rummaged in his pocket for a coin.

Before he could hand it to her, she was bundled away swiftly by a very tall boy with a scar that puckered the skin from his nose to his neck.

'Hey! Whatchya do that for, Stef?' objected Nellie. 'There's a great big bunch of stupid right there, easy pickings. They'd probably even buy that knitted hole you made.'

10

Stef gritted his teeth at her usual gibe about his knitting, but let it pass. 'Bickley's watching.'

Nellie glanced at the window. Sure enough, the pharmacist's face had suddenly loomed behind the grimy glass. He looked about as pleased to see the children as he would have been to see maggots in his breakfast.

She waved at him and yelled, 'Hey, loving the new scam! Didn't think there were any more ways you could get people to pay you for lyin' to 'em, but you found one!'

Stef steered her and Herc further away before Bickley could come out and shout at them for spreading what he called 'fake news' about his shop again. His face had gone purple.

'Nellie! Shhhh! The whole reason we're here is to keep Bickley happy. You can't steal from his customers right under his nose *and* wind him up.'

Nellie snorted. 'Well, I wasn't doing it under his nose till just now. He's been out most of the morning, then hiding in his back room, making 'em drink that stuff and waving his hands over the dregs.' She wiggled her fingers as though performing magic.

Cuthbert and Ashna sauntered over to join them. 'Nellie dear,' Cuthbert said reprovingly. 'I've told you before – you really can't just go up to people and con them out of their money.' Stef nodded vigorously in agreement;

Cuthbert was well versed in legal matters. 'You need to get them to sign a piece of paper first, saying whatever happens next is all their fault. *Then* you can con them.'

'Let's find Tig and go home,' Herc whined. 'I'm tired and there aren't any doughnuts. Besides, my marshmallows will be set by now.'

'I suppose we done our duty. And it *is* getting late,' Nellie agreed, glancing at the sky, which had turned a dingy grey. 'The sun's setting.'

'Don't be daft,' Stef told her. 'It just *feels* like we've been here all day. It can't be much past midday, yet.'

'Well what's that then?' said Herc, pointing triumphantly at the orange tinge on the horizon.

Stef's face was suddenly bloodless, as though his heart had fallen into his boots.

'That's no sunset,' Ashna said, her voice strangled.

The others turned as one towards their home.

A red-orange glow spread across the sky and a large plume of smoke was forming boiling dark clouds above, blotting out the sun.

St Halibut's was on fire.

Chapter Two

'It looks a bit burnt,' Herc observed, as they stood at the very edge of the driveway of St Halibut's the following morning.

Burnt, thought Stef, was an understatement.

Their home was little more than a pile of ash, broken bricks and smouldering stones. He could see familiar shapes – the iron bath, blackened and warped; an empty picture frame that had once housed the holy cheeks of St Halibut herself. But there was no sign of the huge wooden dining table, or any of their beds. They must be among the tiny embers and ash floating around them.

Yesterday it had been right here – solid and forbidding and . . . home. Stef shuddered: they were lucky that none of them had been inside at the time.

There was a cough beside him, and he turned to draw Herc's bandana over the boy's nose and mouth in an attempt to stop him from breathing in the worst of the smoke. He tried to think of something comforting to say, but Herc was peering curiously at a small object he was holding between finger and thumb, misshapen and blackened, crumbling at his touch. 'I *think* it's a bit of marshmallow,' he said, his voice muffled by the bandana. 'But I suppose it could be anything. What if it's a cupboard handle or something? I don't want to eat a cupboard handle.'

Stef sighed. Part of him wanted to shake Herc and ask him if he really didn't see the trouble they were in. They had nowhere to go; just when they had thought everything was perfect, all was lost. There was only desolation and despair for them now.

But desolation and despair never seemed to touch Herc. He tended to ignore them until they went away again. Herc's only concern had been Pamela, but now he knew that the goat was unharmed, he seemed quite content. Her wooden shed had been destroyed – probably by a flying spark from the main fire – but not before Pamela had broken out. She was still wearing a short splintered plank on her horns as a token of her escape, bashing Stef in the ribs every time she turned her head and refusing to let anyone take it off, as though it were a favourite hat.

'I *reckon* it's a burnt marshmallow. Do you think I can still eat it?' Herc asked. 'Or might it be poisonous now?'

'Best not.' Stef watched Cuthbert and Nellie wandering

aimlessly on the other side of the rubble like lost souls. They were picking among the ruins, trying to see if anything could be salvaged. Ashna had stayed below in Sad Sack, because smoke was bad for her damaged lungs, and Tig was keeping her company.

They needed to stick together now, more than ever.

But that was the problem.

They had taken shelter in the Mending House last night, but it was obvious they couldn't stay longer. Despite Maisie's protestations that she'd take care of all six of them, it was painfully clear that there was simply

no room. The dormitories were packed full to bursting already, bunk beds stacked to the ceiling because Maisie couldn't say no to a child sentenced to Mending. If she didn't take them, another Mending House would, and that was a fate no one deserved. Lately, however, saying yes had become literally impossible. It turned out that when you tried to fit three to each bed, two of the occupants ended up falling out. And when they fell on to someone else (because there was no space on the floor either) things could get a little heated.

Last night Stef had wandered around trying to find a clear surface to sleep on and had finally nodded off inside a broom cupboard, leaning against the door frame alongside a mop, which in the morning had turned out to be Cuthbert, who'd had the same idea.

Stef felt tears prick his eyes. A small, warm hand slipped into his. He looked down into Herc's face.

'It'll be all right, you know,' Herc told him solemnly, with a certainty that nearly broke Stef's heart in two. 'We're going to—'

'Uh-oh,' Nellie's voice broke in. 'Here comes the Crooked Chemist.'

Stef glanced where she nodded and his heart sank. Bickley Brimstone's pointy head popped up as he climbed the last few steps to where they stood.

'I heard that,' Bickley puffed. He hadn't been up the hill for many months and clearly didn't have the stamina for it. 'I was about to commiserate with you, offer my sincere condolences for your loss. There's no need for rudeness. What has happened here is a real tragedy.'

Stef gave Nellie a warning frown to quell the sarcastic remark he could see forming on her lips. 'Thanks. We appreciate it, don't we?'

Cuthbert stepped forward briskly and stuck out his hand. 'Ever so kind of you.' Bickley shook it reluctantly, as though it were a wet fish, while Stef gazed at his friend admiringly. Cuthbert's wealthy parents had taught him things like table manners and talking posh when he was very young – skills that Stef had never really been able to see the point of, but at times like this they really came in handy.

Bickley's attention slid expectantly over to Nellie. After a long, mutinous silence, she dredged up a tight smile and a nod so tiny it couldn't have been seen under a microscope.

'Arfur told me the news about Miss Happyday,' Bickley said.

Stef tensed. No doubt Arfur had spun Brimstone a story that hid the fact that the matron had been dead for months, but there was no way of knowing exactly what he'd said. Had he told the pharmacist that she had died in the fire?

'Yeah. It's so sad,' he said, sadly.

'Terribly, awfully sad,' agreed Cuthbert. 'That poor woman. Such a pity.'

Bickley frowned. 'A pity? Suddenly winning thousands of pounds in a beauty contest and abandoning you all for a stellar modelling career? And to do so on the morning of the fire, thereby escaping it! I'd call that an incredible stroke of luck, wouldn't you?'

Arfur had proved himself a true friend, covering for them endlessly. But sometimes he liked to test just how gullible people were. It seemed he hadn't yet reached Bickley's limits.

'Oh, that – yes,' agreed Stef. 'Well, best of luck to her.'

'Never thought she was much of a looker, myself,' said Bickley, who had never seen anything as gorgeous as the handsome fellow who greeted him in the mirror every morning. 'Anyway –' he glanced between the children – 'I came up to let you know that your ride is here. Better not leave them waiting.' He smirked, gesturing down to the bottom of the hill. Where the steps levelled out to the path that led into Sad Sack, there was a large, black-covered carriage attached to a pair of glossy horses.

Stef's skin went cold. Nellie and Cuthbert looked down.

'That's a . . . DEATH carriage,' Cuthbert said blankly.

'Yes. I took the liberty of informing them of your tragic situation. They have found places for you all to live.'

Stef felt Nellie's fingers clutch at his arm.

'Together?' she whispered.

'Don't be silly.' Bickley laughed. 'No, you will be scattered across the country.'

Stef was stunned into silence. Bickley must have put pen to paper to write to DEATH almost the moment the first flames appeared. He stared at the pharmacist and a horrible realization uncoiled in his gut.

It would have taken at least two days for any message to reach DEATH HQ from Sad Sack.

Bickley had not sent it as soon as the fire started.

He had sent it before.

✖ Chapter Three ✖

There was chaos in the town.

Three black-suited DEATH officers were insisting the six homeless St Halibut's children get into the carriage, manhandling them up the step, while Maisie and Ma Yeasty yelled and cried and lamented the fate of the poor innocent orphans. Only Herc seemed unconcerned, leaning against the carriage, still considering his maybe-marshmallow with great concentration. At first, Tig had been glad that her younger brother was coping so well, but now his behaviour seemed bizarre. She feared he was in complete denial about what was happening to them. He could not have realized that Pamela wouldn't be coming with them, for a start. The goat was currently standing guard next to Herc, chewing on a piece of one of the officers' trousers she had claimed when he ventured too close. The officer had gone off to get some carrots from Arty Chokes, in the hope of shifting her. For now, the others had decided to focus on the children who didn't have plank-wearing, horned bodyguards.

'Oh, for shame, for shame!' Maisie was wailing. 'You can't take them so far away and split them up. They won't know a soul. And they talk funny down south – they won't be able to understand a word. Let me take them! I'll build an extension!'

'Madam, it is impossible,' one of the DEATH officers told her firmly. 'You are already past capacity for the Mending House. Perhaps we should check the number of children you currently have in there?'

That shut her up. Officially the Mending House housed forty. In fact, there were more than three times the number of dear darling Poppets than that.

'Oh, Maisie, what can be done?' Ma Yeasty wrung her floury hands. 'I shall never make another doughnut if they go – my heart won't be in it.'

Bickley Brimstone tut-tutted. 'Come, come, ladies. Such fuss! They're going to a better place. Well, a different place. Or rather, lots of different places.' He was exceptionally jolly.

'There's only one thing for it,' Herc announced, oblivious to everything around him. 'I'm going to lick it.'

Nellie was giving the officers a right earful, trying to shock them into backing down. But it was clear that the orphans weren't going to win this fight. DEATH officers with a job to do would not rest until it was done. They were merciless, inevitable, like trapped wind.

Stef allowed himself to be led inside and sat meekly on the bench. Ashna squeezed in beside him, followed by Nellie and Cuthbert. Tig remained, braced against the door frame while an officer tried to squeeze her in. Finally her strength gave way and she fell through, landing on Nellie's lap with an '*Oomph*'. Pamela had wandered off a little way down the street, following the trail of carrots left for her by the quick-thinking officer, and Herc was finally

shepherded into the vehicle, still apparently unconcerned by it all. The doors slammed and they felt the carriage rock as the driver climbed up to her seat.

Bickley's head popped up at the window.

'Goodbye!' he said. 'Have a horrible time! Don't write!'

'You did this,' Nellie seethed. 'You did it on purpose. You've always hated us.'

'What an accusation!' Bickley gasped theatrically.

'It's true!' Stef said. 'You must have told DEATH St Halibut's had burned down at least a day before it actually did. You're telling me that's not suspicious?'

Bickley leaned in. 'I can tell the future, remember? Perhaps you should have asked me what yours held, instead of mocking.'

He grinned, then frowned as his attention was taken by something happening near the driver. His head disappeared from view, and they could hear him talking to the officers. It started quietly, but then there was a shriek from Bickley.

'THIS IS AN OUTRAGE! WILL NOBODY DO THEIR JOB ANYMORE?' He was hoarse with fury.

Suddenly the door to the carriage was wrenched open and an officer yelled, 'Everybody out!'

Dazed and bewildered, the children obediently filed out again. Bickley was arguing furiously with the driver.

'You've trapped the goat *where?*'

Crashing noises from the pharmacy. Breaking glass.

Bickley broke into a run, and made it to his shop just as Pamela sauntered out, her plank knocking out the final shards from the window.

With an enraged growl, Bickley stalked inside and slammed the door behind him, causing the bell to fall off.

Herc had finally popped the marshmallow into his mouth and was now bent over, retching, while Pamela rejoined him, lifting her top lip threateningly at the DEATH officers as they clambered hastily into the carriage.

With a crack of the whip the horses leaped forward, cantering into the distance. As the dust cleared, the children saw a familiar dishevelled figure on the other side of the road.

'Arfur!' Tig gasped. 'What did you do?'

Hands in pockets, Arfur sauntered over, smiling with satisfaction at the disappearing vehicle. 'Just what I said I'd do.' He side-eyed Herc, whose face suggested that even if what was in his mouth had once been a marshmallow, it certainly wasn't now. 'Mate, did you forget to tell 'em?'

Tig put her hands on her hips and turned to her brother. 'Tell us what? You *knew* we weren't actually going?'

Herc didn't speak for a few moments, busy spitting sticky charcoal globules on to the road, his tongue black.

24

'Didn't I say?' he finally managed. 'Arfur's just adopted us.'

'He *what*?' Tig cast a disbelieving eye over Arfur as he waved a wodge of papers in the air. 'The six of us?'

'Nah, nah, don't look like that.' Arfur seemed to read her mind. 'It's just a technical fing to get DEATH off your backs. One or two of them officers owe me, so I pulled in a few favours to get it done on the spot, like. I ain't planning to cook your dinner or darn your socks or run your ruddy baths.'

'Because we don't need baths,' Herc asserted, spitting out the last of the blackened sweet and wiping his mouth with the back of his hand.

'Well . . . thanks,' Tig said, trembling with relief. 'In the nick of time.' Her brother was a menace, but the idea of being away from him for long was unthinkable. He needed her to look out for him or he'd never make it to his next birthday. She reached for Herc's hand and immediately regretted it, covered as it was in sooty saliva.

'Just one thing, though.' Cuthbert raised a finger, always one for details. 'The question of where we live. Because your place is . . .' He hesitated, trying not to give offence. Arfur slept in Maisie's old post cart, which doubled as a mobile library. 'Well, it's rather small,' Cuthbert finished politely.

25

Arfur nodded and clapped a hand on Cuthbert's shoulder. He appeared to be enjoying himself. 'That *is* the question, innit? Lucky for you, I come up wiv a solution last night, while you was all in shock, like. I got somewhere perfect.'

Stef and Tig exchanged a confused glance. 'Really?' Stef asked. 'Near here?'

'Just a hop, skip and a jump away.'

'And it's big enough?' said Tig, hands on hips.

Arfur threw his arms out wide. 'Room for every single one of ya, and more. Running water, lovely views, tucked away so's you won't be disturbed. And that includes by me. I might visit from time to time, but I draw the line at living wiv ya. Ain't got the patience. Or earplugs.'

Tig's brain was turning over and over; it sounded incredible. How could it be possible? Apart from St Halibut's and the Mending House, the nearest large building was the Palatial Hotel ten miles away in Lardidar Valley. Surely Arfur hadn't paid for rooms there?

'Can I tell them?' Herc asked, and bounced with excitement at Arfur's nod. 'We're going *camping*, in the woods! Like Robin Hood!'

✎ Chapter Four ✎

Stef had read all about Robin Hood, of course – there were stories about him in Arfur's mobile library. Mainly they involved twanging bows in daring adventures, sitting around a fire singing songs, and jolly fellowship. But none of them mentioned Robin constantly being interrupted by his friends when trying to go to the toilet in a bush. Robin didn't get woken before dawn every single chuffing morning by a noisy crow right above his head, its caw so sharp it might as well be grating his brain on to a slice of toast. And Robin never had to keep trudging all the way back into town to buy matches because he and his merry men couldn't manage to light fires without them.

Stef felt like they ought to be able to handle that kind of thing, if they were going to be living in the wild now. But he'd tried – they all had – rubbing sticks together at speed in the hope of producing enough heat, or striking

27

stones together to make a spark, and it quickly became clear it just wasn't going to happen. If it had been that easy, he supposed, whoever invented matches wouldn't have bothered. Worse, Sue Perglue was always out of stock at her hardware shop, so Bickley Brimstone's Powders 'n' Potions was the only place they could buy them – it felt awkward to buy matches off the person who had most likely burned down their home.

They had seriously underestimated how much Bickley wanted them out of Sad Sack. Stef had never dreamed that the pharmacist felt so threatened by their presence. Yes, they weren't shy about pointing out that he was a total fraud, but that had never actually harmed his business – it was thriving more than ever.

On moving day, Ma Yeasty had pressed into their hands a large number of paper bags containing, in total, eighteen cinnamon whirls, which had lasted a whole three minutes between them. They always enjoyed Ma Yeasty's delicious pastries – she still hadn't grasped the basics of kitchen hygiene, so the trick was to avoid thinking about where they might have been.

Their little settlement was reached via an overgrown path, which led through the forest from the road. After about an hour's walk the path ended in a large clearing, the darkness of the trees suddenly opening out to reveal an expanse of sky. A freshwater spring bubbled out from a grassy bank – the running water Arfur had promised – and trickled away a little distance into the trees before being absorbed back into the boggy ground to one side.

After the initial shock, Ashna had cast her eye over the clearing and announced that the place had potential. With a bit of work, they might be happy here. And they'd be together, which was all that really mattered. Nellie, who was a town girl at heart, liked to complain about the lack of facilities, but even she couldn't hide the fact that she was enjoying herself. They were all perfectly settled. Except, maybe, for Stef.

He was missing home comforts. It wasn't that he didn't like nature; he just didn't want it crawling up his trouser leg or burrowing into his hair or biting him in the armpit. Ashna, who knew a lot about insects and plants, assured him there was nothing that could really hurt him, but that wasn't the point.

They had spent the first few nights in hastily constructed shelters made from fallen branches and leaves interwoven with mud and grass, but these had been so uncomfortable – and wet, after a night's rain – that it had spurred all the orphans to work. Arfur provided some planks and nails – though he refused to say where he'd got them – and with the help of diagrams from some of his DIY books, they had upgraded the shelters into rough huts. They'd even got some rubber sheeting from Sue Perglue, which they used on the roofs to keep the rain off. There was now a circle of stones at the centre of the clearing, within which they made the fire, and Ashna had rigged up a tripod of long sticks to hang a cooking pot from. Slowly, their home was taking shape. It wasn't exactly the Palatial Hotel, but it was all right.

Stef had just finished another hut, but it had turned out wonky again. It was so dispiriting. His friends' efforts were no better, but they didn't seem to care. They had lost interest in building, once the basics were done. But Stef cared. What would it be like in winter, for a start? Proper houses had insulation, and windows, and doors, and other modern knick-knacks that stopped you from inconveniently freezing to death, but he didn't know how to make those. If only someone would come and give him a few pointers, lend him some tools and explain how to use them, maybe he could become good at it. Now that would be something. It would certainly be better than knitting.

Anything was better than knitting.

Arfur, true to his word, had barely hung around at all – he'd been as horrified as they were about the idea of actually parenting them. So they would fend for themselves, just as they'd done at St Halibut's – forming their own family. Back there, they had divided the tasks between them, according to their strengths – Tig had taken the lead, it was true, but Stef had known he was needed. The dependable one. The one who would listen to everybody's worries and make them feel better. The one who could reach the top shelf in the kitchen. He, Tig and Herc had been an inseparable trio.

But something had shifted since they had arrived in their new home; Stef couldn't shake the sense he had stepped through a door for a moment and somehow got locked out.

They were all his friends, of course, but the previously tight bonds between them felt loose, insecure. Tig never seemed to seek him out anymore, and the chemistry of their friendship had changed. Tig was constantly telling Herc off, and Herc was busy with his marshmallows and Pamela, and they both barely noticed Stef at all. Ever since they had escaped the Mending House by the tiniest of margins, it was as though Tig were trying to predict every possible danger, every conceivable trouble Herc might get into, and prevent it. It was true that her brother could get a bit . . . dangerously inventive, sometimes. He just needed some guidance, but Tig was clamping down on every little thing. She was not so much his sister as his prison warden.

Stef could hear them arguing now.

★

'It's not fair! Why does everyone else get to design their own huts, but I'm not allowed to?'

Tig felt her temper rising. 'Because your ideas are ridiculous. And will you come out, please? I can't talk to you properly while you're in there.' Herc was inside the newest hut. He already had his own to sleep in, but he had commandeered this one too, and pinned a thick rubber sheet across the door gap. A torn scrap of paper stuck to it read *KEP OWT*.

'I'm busy. Why can't we build *my* design? It's from a book, same as yours.'

'Mine was from a *serious* book. The house in yours is completely crazy. For the last time: you can't live in a hole halfway up that dead oak tree and build a spiral slide down inside the trunk. We should probably cut it down, actually, before it falls.' She gazed up into the branches nervously.

'Exactly – it's dead already, so I wouldn't be hurting it. We just need to support it. And it's not just the tree slide, I have loads of other ideas. You saw the drawings I did. It's all planned out.'

He had spent hours perfecting his 'architectural designs' and a proposed map of the clearing; when complete, the whole thing was every bit as deranged as she had feared.

32

Pamela raised her head and stopped mid-chomp for a moment to blink unnervingly at Tig. The goat had discovered a taste for the chamomile flowers that dotted the clearing, and was chewing on them with a blissful expression most unlike her usual venomous glare. She hadn't bitten or headbutted anyone lately, but that could change at any time. Herc was the only person who was always entirely safe with her. She had finally allowed him to remove the broken plank from her horns, and he had somehow persuaded her to wear a pink collar so that he could lead her around, though she managed to make it look menacing.

The unmistakeable crackle of lit twigs reached Tig. A curl of smoke was rising from the roof, and there was a strange, sweet smell. 'Herc!' Tig slapped the wall of the hut and it wobbled. 'I can see smoke! You've set a fire, haven't you?'

There was silence, and then a small but defiant voice. 'I haven't. It's . . . fog. Just a very small bit.'

She put her hands on her hips. 'I am *not* messing about. If you don't tell me, I'll get Stef to knock this place down and make you a cage instead.'

There was a loud sigh, and then Herc's head appeared through the crack in the door. His face was sooty. 'Look. It's not dangerous. OK, so I admit I've got a fire going.

But it's completely safe. Stef made a smoke hole in the roof for me, like they used to in medieval times. We saw a picture of one in another book. A *serious* book.'

She sighed. People made out like books were a good thing, but then most of them hadn't seen the hare-brained schemes they could inspire in Herc's brain. And she'd have to have a word with Stef about indulging her brother's every demand – they needed to restrain him, not encourage him.

Tig threw out her hands in frustration. 'But *why* have you made a fire in there, when there's already one out here? I need to know.'

He shook his head. 'No, you *want* to know. That's completely different. You're not my mum.'

This was a new phrase. Herc had begun to deploy it whenever Tig asked him to do anything, or *not* to do anything. She had wondered if it meant he was pining somehow for the mother they had never known. But if it was mothering he wanted, it wasn't the sort that stopped him embarking on risky experiments or demanded he eat vegetables.

'Herc, so help me, I will rip that sheet off its nails and drag you out of there by your ankles.'

A pause. 'I'm making marshmallows.' He stuck his hand through the gap again and handed something spongy to her, still warm: a small, white marshmallow. She sniffed it suspiciously. It

smelt quite good – vaguely fruity. 'Ma Yeasty gave me everything I need. They're still not right, but I'm getting better at them. You have to melt the sugar and—'

He went off on a long, detailed explanation of how he was perfecting the recipe, and she heard the enthusiasm, the happiness in his voice. He'd been crushed when she'd dismissed his ridiculous plans for their little village. Her mind ran over all the things he might do instead of cooking sweets, things he *had* done in the past. At least he wasn't manufacturing explosives, or exploring sewage. It would keep him from hogging the main fire they needed for cooking meals. It would stop him wandering aimlessly into Sad Sack searching for excitement and, when he couldn't find any, causing some.

'Well . . . just promise me you'll make sure someone else – someone older – is around nearby before you set the fire, OK? And put it out before you leave the hut. You know what happened to St Halibut's. You've seen what fire can do.'

'That wasn't my fault!' He pouted. 'Honestly. I'm not *stupid*. You're even meaner than Miss Happyday.' He disappeared back inside in a huff.

Making her way back through the clearing, Tig popped the marshmallow in her mouth.

Hmm, she thought. Not bad at all.

✌ Chapter Five ✌

Bickley Brimstone had heard the saying that the customer was always right. Clearly, whoever came up with it had never encountered the customers in his shop.

He waited in his back room for Ralph Cornswallop the farmer to sip his tea, and reflected sadly on what a terrible and lonely burden it was to be the only person in town with any sense. Bickley's customers were often so deeply in the wrong you couldn't have dug them out with a shovel and a team of rescue dogs. And the worst of it was that he couldn't tell them so to their faces because he wanted them to keep giving him cash.

It made running a shop very depressing. It wasn't what he'd planned for his life. There had been a time when power and influence awaited; it just turned out they'd been waiting for someone else. He had so many useful skills: he was intolerant, demanding, rigid and nit-picking, unbothered by self-doubt. He'd have had a wonderful career in the Ministry of FUN (Forms, Underlining and Notices), if only they'd given him a chance. Unfortunately they hadn't, because he'd smudged his signature on the application form. They would suffer for that, eventually. One day, when he was in charge of the world, FUN would rue the day they had rejected him.

And so he had become a pharmacist, or rather, pharmac-ish . . . He'd never gone to the trouble of actually training, and his fake certificates were proudly displayed on the wall for all to see: chemistry, botany, biology, apology. That last one was meant to say *acology* – the study of medical remedies – but the calligrapher's hand had slipped and the scoundrel had refused a refund. Not that it mattered – his customers hadn't a clue.

He'd been certain that fortune telling and miracle healing were the answer to his problems. They used the one thing Sad Sackers were good at – being total suckers – and made money from it.

It wasn't turning out to be that simple, though.

'I dunno,' said Cornswallop, 'I'm just not sure I wanna, you know, go into the future. I've got responsibilities here—'

'Mm, heh heh.' Bickley gave a polite chuckle. 'I see I have not made myself clear. The tea does not transport you

38

into the future. That would be s—' He stopped, putting the brakes on the word 'stupid' at the last moment. Sad Sackers might be gullible, but they were quick to spot an insult. '. . . scientifically impossible. No, no, the tea merely *reveals*. It shows us a picture, if you like. There is no . . . *time travel*.'

'Ahhh.' Cornswallop's brow cleared. 'So I picture an animal, in my head, like, and you tell me what I'm thinking. Like a sheep. Except not a sheep, cos I just told you. Maybe a cow. Except not that now, either.'

Bickley ground his teeth together in an effort not to swear. 'Mr Cornswallop, I fear you have misunderstood the purpose of this appointment. I do not read your mind. You drink the tea, and what lies ahead will be revealed.' He indicated the china cup before him.

'Well I never! Talkin' tea, is it?' Cornswallop leaned over so his nose was nearly in the steaming liquid, and spoke loudly and slowly. 'WHAT . . . DAY . . . WILL . . . IT . . . BE . . . TOMORROW?' He winked at the pharmacist and tapped his nose knowingly, then whispered, 'That's a test question, see, 'bout the future. If it gets that right, we'll know we can trust it.'

Bickley's lip curled, though his moustache remained dead horizontal, as if it had its own suspension. 'It doesn't *speak*, you utter –' he checked himself with a monumental

39

effort, and took a long, shuddering breath – '*customer*. Just DRINK.'

There was a slurping noise as the farmer tipped the cup.

A second or two of quiet. Then an arc of tea left Cornswallop's mouth at great speed. 'BLLLEEEURGH! Tastes like pee! Oh. Look at that. Sorry about your shirt.'

Bickley rose abruptly and excused himself to change upstairs, mainly to stop himself smashing the teapot over Cornswallop's head.

Up in the flat, he let his gaze drift up to St Halibut's hill.

It was satisfying to see the emptiness at the top where the mansion had always stood.

When it had happened, over a month ago now, the residents of Sad Sack were all running about frantically as though something might be done. But of course it could not; the fire service was sixteen miles to the west in Great Numpton, and Queenie the fire marshal only worked Wednesdays and Fridays. She insisted on being booked in advance so she had a chance to put her teeth in. Also, her bucket leaked.

He had never intended to kill them when he set the fire, of course – he wasn't a *monster*. He had graciously provided the Sad Sack Festival to ensure they were all out.

It was better than they deserved. He had recently discovered that the children had been matronless for months; that Miss Happyday had not in fact won a beauty contest, and was not dead quiet but dead *dead*. They had all been lying to him the whole time. Laughing at him.

Did they think he was just going to put up with them openly mocking his new services? And that Nellie girl, stealing from his customers! How dare she? That was *his* job. He wasn't just going to sit by while those dimwits ruined his business.

The fire was meant to ensure they would be sent far away, where they could no longer besmirch his reputation, and that of his business. It was one thing not to believe in his remedies themselves, but quite another to walk around town mocking him publicly. People might stop buying from him.

It was Arfur's fault they were still hanging around . . . that swindler who had tried his hand at every dodgy scam going, and now carted around a mobile library full of trashy books. He must have adopted the orphans purely to annoy Bickley. Infuriatingly, DEATH had instantly washed their hands of the matter. *Not our problem anymore*, they'd said. Not even when Arfur set the children up in Knott Wood. Brimstone had watched the young twerps carrying rolls of rubber sheeting, saws and hammers down the road, and wondered what they were up to. He had barely been able to believe his ears when he'd heard where they were living. It was entirely unacceptable.

Bickley was not the sort of person to so easily give up on a grudge. He'd escalated the matter to FUN. If you could count it, measure it, see it, imagine it, even sneeze it, they had a form for it. Maybe they'd finally realize what a terrible mistake they'd made in failing to give him a job.

But to his dismay, his sixteen-page complaint to FUN had been passed from department to department, each declaring that it wasn't precisely their area, until it had been returned to him with a sticky note asking if he had thought about reporting them to DEATH, instead. It was entirely typical – the two ministries overlapped and no one was ever sure if something was a FUN problem, or a DEATH one. Usually it was decided by playing a game of hot potato. Conversely, they fought to be in charge of the good stuff – anything involving celebrities, or events where there would be cocktail sausages on sticks.

FUN was already on Brimstone's revenge list. Along with – among others – DEATH, the orphans, Arfur, Arfur's pigeons, the Sad Sack Croquet Club, his Year 8 PE teacher, people who asked for receipts, ladybirds, and Miss Happyday (being dead wasn't nearly enough to strike her off the list). But after the business with the orphans he

had underlined the FUN acronym twice more and circled it so hard the pencil broke.

He just needed a little patience; change was coming.

In fact, if his sources were correct, change was arriving today.

He heard a soft cooing coming from outside. As always, several of Arfur's infernal pigeons were squatting on the window sill, staring insolently at him. They had already covered the shop sign of Powders 'n' Potions with vile streams of brown muck so that the sign now read *OW–N PO–O–S*.

He rapped smartly on the window to scare the pigeons

off, and they all emptied their bowels in surprise.

As if that wasn't enough, he spotted one of the wretched orphans on the high street, looking horribly like he might be thinking about entering the shop.

Fists clenched, Bickley headed back down to Cornswallop.

The pharmacy was empty when Stef stepped inside.

A headache nagged at his temples, set off by the pungent scent of all the herbs, tobacco and strange chemicals on the shelves of Powders 'n' Potions. He tried to breathe shallowly, but found that made him dizzy, so he resigned himself to the nasty thick taste in his throat and decided to browse while he waited for Bickley Brimstone to appear from the back room.

The door that led to it was slightly ajar, and through the gap he could see the pharmacist drumming his fingers on the desk while Ralph Cornswallop drank something from a small china cup.

Stef's discomfort ratcheted up a notch. There was a bell on the desk whose label invited customers to ring for attention, but from experience, it was best not to use it. Bickley did not like to be – as he put it – 'summoned like a genie to grant your pathetic wishes'.

Stef thought about heading back to the woods, without

the matches he'd come for. But Ashna was at this moment buying pastries in Ma Yeasty's, and if *he* didn't get the matches she'd march in here fearlessly and get them herself, and he'd never live it down.

Being in here brought back horrible memories of the fire. If only he could get the images out of his head: smoke billowing over the mansion, their home a charcoal smudge against the summer sky high above, and inside, a pulsing, ravenous energy consuming the building. Flames licking hungrily up the stone walls, making them shimmer like glass. Tongues of fire flickering from the upstairs windows until with a sharp thud, the dormitory window had shattered as they stood there, and flames poured out of it, sparks flying in every direction . . .

'Well? What are you doing skulking around, boy?'

He snapped back to the present and found Bickley's face two inches from his own, his minty breath blasting tears from Stef's eyes. The front door clicked closed as Cornswallop shut it on his way out.

'I . . . uh . . . just wanted some matches.' He handed over his coin.

'How about a "please"? Or is that too much trouble? Your new *father* lets you speak to him like that, does he?' Brimstone clambered on to the stool slowly, huffing and puffing crossly as though he were a thousand years old.

'And don't think I don't know what's going on, lad. You're hanging around in Knott Wood, where you shouldn't be.'

A box of matches hit Stef in the chest before dropping into his hands. Bickley climbed down, fixing him with a sharp look. 'You want to watch out. There's wild creatures in there that will tear you to pieces given half a chance.'

Stef nodded absently. Pamela did fit that description, but she'd been calmer lately – Ashna's theory was that eating the chamomile was making her a little bit more relaxed. As for any other wild creatures, well, he doubted there were any foolhardy enough to approach the camp with her guarding it.

Bickley's voice was now a malicious hiss, and Stef had to lean in to hear him. 'You should get out while you can. Before it's too late. Your doom approaches, boy.' The pharmacist's eyes were veined with red, his pupils large; it was hard to look away.

Stef knew that Bickley was just trying to scare him. It was nonsense – just part of the ridiculous man's massive grudge against them. So why was his own throat suddenly dry, his skin clammy with fear?

A tinkling tune came from the back room, a clock striking. It broke the moment and finally freed Stef's frozen legs.

Time to get out.

46

'Well, thanks for the matches,' Stef blurted. He took a few steps running before remembering this was best done facing forwards, so he twisted and barged straight into the door, nose crunching against the glass. Slippery-fingered, he grabbed the handle and yanked it open successfully on the third attempt. He finally felt the sweet breath of fresh air on his face, just before a high-pitched whinny split his eardrums.

He caught a glimpse of a carriage, the whites of the horse's eyes looming just before it slammed into his body.

❧ Chapter Six ❧

*T*he loaf of bread looked delicious. Apart from the fact that it was squashed at one end, where Ma Yeasty had gripped it, and there were five deep indentations where her fingers had broken through the crust. They hadn't been there a few minutes ago, but a fly had buzzed into the shop and Ma Yeasty had made the loaf her weapon of choice for swatting the thing. After several failed attempts to get it when it landed on the counter, the floor, the wall, and her own leg, she had finally vanquished it with a hefty swipe through mid-air, sending the insect tumbling into a line of flans with a tiny *plop*.

She handed the loaf to Ashna with a satisfied nod. 'Nasty thing. Carry germs, they do.' Ashna was pretty sure there were more germs under a single one of Ma Yeasty's fingernails than in the entire fly population of Sad Sack, but didn't want to hurt her feelings. She would just cut that end off the loaf when she got back to Marshmallow – the name Herc had insisted on giving their new home, and which no one had the energy to argue with.

Ma Yeasty continued to hum the odd little tune she had broken off from, the same six notes up and down, over and over again, while checking on the dough rising behind her in the kitchen. She was a talented baker, less so singer, unless you enjoyed the sound of a catfight bouncing down a flight of stairs inside bagpipes. She bustled back in and stopped long enough to ask cheerfully, 'How are you doing, my love? Having fun camping?'

'It's all proper, now, Ma Yeasty. You should see it. It's like a little village.'

The baker smiled. 'Need anything else?'

'No, thanks. Stef's getting matches from Powders 'n' Potions, so I said I'd wait here for him and we'll walk back together.'

A soft expression came over Ma Yeasty, as though her face were melting. 'That man! Who'd have thought it?'

'Stef?'

Ma Yeasty laughed. 'No, dear, Stef's not a man, just a lovely big bear of a boy. I'm talking about Bickley Brimstone! Always had him down as a bit of a berk, but my, that tea he makes! Cor, it can do anything. You know old Rhona Lumpendorf's toe?'

'Er . . .'

'Few weeks back, it were all big and red and sore with this sorta yellow stuff oozing . . .'

Ashna tried not to listen as Ma Yeasty described the unfortunate toe in great detail.

'. . . and then she went and had some of Bickley's tea, and do you know what?' Ma Yeasty slapped her hands on the counter to emphasize her point. 'It got better! An act-chu-al miracle!'

'What, there and then?' This would indeed be news – a Powders 'n' Potions remedy actually doing something it claimed to do?

Ma Yeasty blinked. 'Well, no, it was a couple of weeks later, sort of gradual, like. Amazing, eh?'

Ashna couldn't muster the enthusiasm to look amazed, but just about managed mildly interested. Unfortunately, that seemed to encourage Ma Yeasty.

'And he told me my fortune, you know – made me tea, then told me what's what. It was brilliant.'

'Came true, did it?'

Ma Yeasty hesitated. 'Well, not yet.'

'What did he say was going to happen?'

The baker opened her mouth to reply, and then closed it, with a look of great concentration. 'Do you know, I can't actually remember. That's funny. I could have sworn he . . .'

She trailed off, then tried again. 'It was the way he . . . like, when he . . . so, you know, well worth the money.'

'Sounds like it,' Ashna said, suppressing a smirk.

'He had this huge book what he'd been reading. You should see the size of it. Dunno what it was about, but it was *that big*, with itty-bitty writing. That's how you know it's something intelligent, see? Must've been his fortune-telling-miracle-performing-tea guide.'

Ashna pulled a face; she'd never seen Bickley with a book before. He always sneered at the comics in Arfur's library. Whatever this book was, he was probably using it to stand on to reach high shelves.

Ma Yeasty frowned and shook her head, distracted. 'Anyway, want some doughnuts as well? Special offer. Fifty per cent off. Oh, who am I kidding – they're free to you lot.' She winked.

'Uh, yeah, OK. Thanks. I thought you didn't even like Bickley?'

Ma Yeasty began to put the doughnuts in a paper bag. 'I don't know about that. But he must've been hiding his talents. Look at all the good he's doing now! And he's won all sorts of awards, you know.'

This was too much. 'He's wins *one* award every year, and he gives that to himself. We're pretty sure it was him that burned down St Halibut's!'

Ma Yeasty gasped. 'Now Ashna, you mustn't keep saying that. You've given no evidence whatsoever, and you can ruin an innocent person's life by going round talking that way. Nobody here would have done such an awful thing.'

'He's not innocent. Don't be so gullible.' As it came out of her mouth, Ashna realized it sounded ruder than she had intended.

Ma Yeasty's mouth pursed and a sharpness came into her eyes. 'Well, I'm sure I'm not as clever as *some*.'

'Sorry, Ma Yeasty, I didn't mean . . . Sorry.'

The atmosphere in the bakery had soured all of a sudden. Ma Yeasty was normally the first to laugh at Bickley Brimstone's absurdities; she'd always liked to find the best in people, but this was disturbing.

Ashna thanked her again for the doughnuts and left.

There was no sign of Stef yet. There had been some kind of kerfuffle outside Powders 'n' Potions while she was in the bakery, though it seemed to be over now. Just before the bakery door closed, Ashna heard Ma Yeasty humming that little tune again.

She could not believe for a second that Bickley Brimstone had any hidden good qualities. If so, they weren't just hard to see, they were buried underground somewhere *very* remote, their location expertly camouflaged. But the residents of Sad Sack seemed to be accepting his every word. She thought back to the queue outside his shop at the festival and her niggling discomfort increased. He was telling all those people *something* – and it was obviously a scam . . . but what, exactly?

Ma Yeasty was awfully trusting. It would not be hard to take advantage of her.

Ashna put it to the back of her mind and decided not to worry about it. If the orphans were capable of taking care of themselves, then grown-ups should be, too.

❧ Chapter Seven ❧

A woman was gently dabbing at Stef's temple with a piece of gauze, her face full of deep concern.

He tried to focus on her, and pain shot across the back of his head. He could feel giant bruises bubbling up under the skin all over his body.

'That was a very brave thing you did out there,' she said. She was crouched next to him – pale skinned, with blonde curls that bounced like springs as she nodded, wearing an expensive-looking blue dress with yellow daisies on it and a matching blue hat, angled slightly to one side. A shimmering necklace reflected the light from the window and half dazzled him. On her fingers, an array of sparkling jewels. A pleasant lavender scent hung about her.

'Thanks,' Stef muttered, without the faintest clue what she was talking about.

'The way you threw yourself in front of my taxicab when it was out of control, and stopped it with your body. So courageous!'

When she put it like that, getting run over sounded kind of heroic.

He shifted painfully and sat up. He was on the floor of Powders 'n' Potions; he must have been carried back inside. 'How long was I out?'

'Only a few minutes,' she reassured him. 'Bickley, give this boy a drink of water.' Stef winced, awaiting the tirade of fury that would surely follow this request. But to his astonishment, Brimstone grabbed the footstool behind the counter, leaped up like a gazelle to reach a clear bottle, filled a glass from it and scampered round to present it to the woman as though it were the Sad Sack Business Association Trophy.

'Of course, of course,' Bickley said, 'though he looks fine to me. Completely fine,' he added, in a tone that suggested he'd like to do something about that.

Stef took the water, sniffed it to be sure, and downed it. 'Can you stand?'

He could. His temple throbbed, and he felt as though . . . well, as though he'd been run over by a horse. He'd been incredibly lucky not to have been killed. Although also incredibly unlucky to end up in its path, since there were hardly any vehicles in Sad Sack, except for Arfur's mobile library, which Maisie's pony Bernard pulled along at a terrifying four miles per hour. 'Thanks. I'll be OK.'

'Amazing!' she said. 'You really are made of strong stuff!'

The pharmacist looked like he might puke at this. 'Anyway,' Bickley said, 'as I was saying before the boy woke up, may I *emphasize* once again how utterly delighted, nay, honoured, I am to meet you, Ms Crumplepatch.'

The name rang a faint bell in Stef's head, but he couldn't place it.

'I'd rather you didn't,' she answered smoothly. 'I came in for a headache remedy.'

Bickley's face collapsed as though this were the worst news he had ever heard and he'd probably never get over it. 'Oh! Poor, poor you. I am *so* sorry to hear you have a headache. Does it hurt *very* much?'

Stef could not believe his ears. He had never heard the grumpy pharmacist express sympathy before, except sarcastically. What had happened to him? He watched as Bickley bustled around finding remedies for his customer to choose from.

'I'm just too busy, as usual,' she was saying. 'So much to organize with this project. I'm at the end of my tether trying to find people who will turn up on time and do a full day's work. I've had to get people in from three counties just to get started, and it's still not enough. And on top of that I've got this awful little man from FUN following me around, checking the equipment and asking silly questions.' She rolled her eyes. 'He could talk the hind leg off a donkey. No wonder I've got a headache.'

'Oh, *FUN*.' Bickley shuddered. 'I sympathize, madam. I myself have suffered similar . . .'

As Bickley moaned on about the wickedness of FUN and how they rejected all the best people when they applied for jobs, the woman winked at Stef and he found himself smiling back. At once he remembered where he had heard the name: Crumplepatch Industries – one of the largest and most successful companies in the country, with headquarters in Rankshire. There were many branches: Crumplepatch Coal Mines, Crumplepatch Railways, Crumplepatch Steelworks, Crumplepatch Cabbies, Crumplepatch Crumpets, to name but a few.

'Your project is in Sad Sack?' he asked, trying to hide his astonishment. No decent company had ever been interested in the town before.

Bickley abruptly interrupted his own diatribe on FUN, flapping at Stef as though he were a fly about to land on his lunch. 'This is Benadrylla Crumplepatch! You can't just *talk* to her. You are in the presence of the greatest businesswoman ever to set foot in Garbashire! Madam: I'm so sorry that you have been subjected to this boy's

58

ignorance. But now that you're here, can I tempt you to a cup of tea? Your headache will be gone in no time. Or I could tell your fortune, perhaps? No doubt I can reveal something that will help you.'

Stef wanted to retort that she probably already knew that night time would be followed by morning, but held his tongue.

Benadrylla shook her head politely as she took the headache remedy. The bottle clinked against her rings as she dropped it into a pocket of her dress. 'Not today, thank you, Mr Bumscone. Or may I call you Bickspee?'

The pharmacist winced. 'You . . . you may. Although the name's actually—'

'I don't have time to sit down for tea. Perhaps another occasion. It sounds *fascinating*, though.' She caught Stef's eye, her lips twitched, and he had the sense that she was sharing a private joke with him. Her gaze lingered on his scar, and he felt his face grow hot. 'So I hear you're living in Knott Wood, Stef?'

Oh, great. What else had Bickley told her while he was unconscious? Her stare was so penetrating, he had to look at the floor instead. 'Yes. It's all legal, though.' He remembered what Cuthbert had told them to say if anyone asked. 'There are no regulations against people living in woods.'

'It's a legal loophole that ought to be shut,' Bickley snapped.

'Well, it's open,' Stef said, and then, worrying about sounding rude, he added, 'Sorry.'

Benadrylla was smiling with one side of her mouth, as though all this amused her. 'I see you are well versed in these matters. You're absolutely right. That's the sort of creative thinking I admire. All obstacles can be overcome, with persistence.'

Brimstone made a huffing snort that suggested he had an opinion, but he didn't venture it.

'What sort of project is it?' Stef asked. He hoped for Ma Yeasty's sake she wasn't planning to set up a branch of Crumplepatch Crumpets – Sad Sackers would probably jump at the chance to buy pastries that hadn't been sat on or sneezed in; they'd desert Ma Yeasty in droves.

Bickley couldn't resist demonstrating his superior knowledge. 'Don't you know anything? Crumplepatch

Railways is working to connect Sad Sack to the rest of the world!'

This was news to Stef. 'We're getting a railway? Where's it going?'

Bickley opened his mouth to reply but Benadrylla talked right over him. 'All the way to Little Wazzock, around Knott Wood, following the road.'

This was a surprise. It would be hard to imagine a more dismal destination; Little Wazzock was practically abandoned. Last time he'd been there it had been home to a single family – of rats. It made Sad Sack look like a bustling metropolis.

Stef's sceptical expression offended Bickley. 'Little Wazzock is just the beginning,' he snapped. 'Insolent boy.'

Benadrylla gave Bickley a quelling stare and explained to Stef gently, 'Eventually, I shall have a coal mine there – I only have one at the moment, and there is a great deal of coal to be found in this area. That will mean many, many jobs for people in Sad Sack. But Little Wazzock, and indeed this entire area, is rather remote.' This was an understatement – people elsewhere tended to forget that Garbashire existed. 'So first, we need infrastructure. Do you know what that means? A way to get things there, and back out again. Transport for equipment, people, horses, and of course the coal. When this section of track is built, we will connect it up to the other tracks that are already being built, all the way up to my headquarters in Rankshire.'

Bickley rubbed his hands. 'Imagine, all those people visiting Sad Sack. They'll need pharmaceuticals when they get here, I expect.'

Stef didn't doubt it. Sad Sack was enough to make anyone ill.

'We start work building the station tomorrow morning, just at the edge of town, and the first set of tracks will be laid out as far as the crossroads shortly after. I'm about to set up a temporary camp for my workers in the fields there.'

Bickley leaned forward to insert himself between them. 'If you need any help, Ms Crumplepatch, my local knowledge is second to none—'

She talked over him again and addressed herself to Stef instead. 'I wonder . . .' Benadrylla said, 'if you might like to be involved, Stef? I could do with someone like you.'

'Involved?' Stef could barely believe she was suggesting what it sounded like she was suggesting. *A job?* Before he could tell himself not to get excited, the idea sprouted and blossomed in his mind, an answer to his prayers. 'Involved with the railway, you mean?'

Bickley was barely containing his fury at the way the conversation had rattled right past him as though he weren't there, so he made a desperate attempt to board it. 'Oh, very amusing, madam! And what a beautiful flowery dress you're wearing. Are those daisies? Delightful. Anyway, as I was saying, I've always thought that Sad Sack must be dragged kicking and screaming into the modern world, and Crumplepatch Railways is just the right—'

'Hmm,' mused Benadrylla, rolling her necklace between her fingers and considering Stef thoughtfully. Her voice, quiet as it was, steamrollered over Brimstone. 'Come by tomorrow, Stef, when I have considered how we can best fulfil your potential. You can find me in the camp, by the crossroads. It'll go up fast – you won't be able to miss it by the morning.'

His face felt warm and tingly. 'Thanks. I . . . I will.'

He left them in the pharmacy and began hobbling towards Ashna, whom he could see waiting further up the street with a bulging paper bag. Her face creased into alarm at the state of him, and she raged all the way home that if she hadn't been in Ma Yeasty's and missed the accident she would have given the cab driver a piece of her mind.

But Stef felt energized, despite the cuts and bruises, and the venomous glare Bickley had given him on the way out. For the first time, someone had looked at him and seen not an overgrown, clumsy child whose main talent was blocking sunlight, but someone who could be useful.

Benadrylla Crumplepatch saw potential in him, and he couldn't remember the last time anyone had done that.

✎ Chapter Eight ✎

'o you lot think there's anything odd about Ma Yeasty lately?' Ashna asked, carefully finishing off a purl stitch on her scarf. Her missing finger didn't seem to matter when she was knitting; it still wasn't her favourite thing to do, but something about the repetitive motions helped her to think.

Nellie glanced up from where she was sitting cross-legged on the grass with the others, whittling at a long stick with a pocketknife. 'Yeah, course.'

'No, I don't mean the usual. Not the sneezing into wraps and bum-scratching with the bakery tongs. I mean her . . . attitude, sort of thing. She's changed.'

'Oh.' Nellie gave it some thought. Ma Yeasty's attitude to kitchen hygiene was much the same as it always had been. Worse, if anything; last week Stef had watched her wipe mud off the floor with a croissant and replace it on its tray without even dusting it off.

Ashna shrugged. 'It's probably nothing. Doesn't matter.'

Cuthbert looked up from his knitting – an intricately patterned all-in-one garment with frills and ruffs and buttons and pleats so complicated that it would surely need its own set of instructions for how to wear it. 'Nellie, aren't you meant to be making that jumper?'

Nellie shrugged. 'I guess. Maisie don't seem to be in a hurry for it. Too hot to wear it for a few months, anyway. And she paid me for that fing I gave her last week.'

Ashna frowned. 'You didn't make anything last week.'

'Exackly. I just gave her back the ball of wool and she says it were a good effort and give me a penny. So what's the point? She paid Stef an' all, for . . . I mean, I don't even know what that was meant to be.'

'A sock,' Stef muttered gloomily. He didn't understand how Nellie could be so unbothered about not producing anything useful. It was eating him up.

He was never going to feel passionate about knitting, like Cuthbert. But he liked the idea of building things, and had tried to make the place look nice; he'd even carved a little sign at the entrance to the clearing. *Marshmallow*, it said, in spidery lettering. Except the knife had slipped at the end and scratched his thigh. And, according to Cuthbert, he'd spelled it wrong. The sign looked rubbish and he'd had to bandage his leg. If only he could learn how to craft these things . . . But there was no one to teach him, and he could only get so far by learning from books.

'A sock, yeah. Wiv no hole to get yer foot in!' Nellie snorted with laughter.

'Pamela can make a hole in it, if you like,' Herc offered helpfully. 'It's no trouble. She likes doing it.' This was true. Anyone who stood too close to her for long was liable to find their clothes had a few extra buttonholes, sometimes an extra armhole.

'Comes to something when Pamela has to fix Stef's mistakes.' Tig chuckled. 'How does it feel to be shown up by a goat?'

Cuthbert nudged her reproachfully, and she relented. 'Just kidding, Stef. You're getting better at it.'

This was clearly untrue. And irritating. He hated it when they lied to make him feel better. It didn't work. In fact, it made him feel worse.

A week had passed since his meeting with Benadrylla; his bruises were healed, but still he hadn't gone to see her. After that first heady rush of excitement, reality had settled in. What could he possibly have to offer Benadrylla Crumplepatch? He didn't have any skills or knowledge. She'd got the wrong idea about him because of the accident. He wouldn't even be able to meet her eye, knowing he

66

was a fraud. He'd told the others about the railway, of course – and now they could see the work for themselves whenever they left the woods – but he hadn't mentioned meeting Benadrylla. Somehow the more he thought about her words, the more ridiculous they seemed. He must have misunderstood; she was just being kind.

He looked up; somebody was standing at the clearing entrance. For a moment, he thought she must be just in his mind – an image of Benadrylla Crumplepatch that he had summoned by thinking of her. But then the others sprang up, alarmed.

'It's all right, children!' She held out her palms reassuringly. 'You're not in trouble. I just came to see your wonderful abode for myself. I've heard terrible things about it from the pharmacist in Sad Sack, so I *knew* it must be good.'

She wandered among them, gazing admiringly around. She was wearing a different flowery dress today, one with red silken petals against a cream background. It swished against the grass as she walked. Stef was mesmerized, scrabbling to his feet only when she stood right in front of him.

'Oh, this is *charming*.' She clapped her hands. 'Look what a lovely little camp you've made! So quirky! I adore it.'

Only then did Stef notice the boy who followed just behind her. The boy had a sceptical expression that made it clear 'charming' was not the word he'd have chosen. He was carrying a huge wicker basket covered with a cloth. Benadrylla gestured at it. 'I brought you some things to cheer you all up. Just a few bits and pieces.'

Nellie was standing with her hands on her hips, warily. 'Just a sec, lady. Can we go back a bit? Who the blazes are you?'

Benadrylla laughed, her hands to her face. 'Oh! Silly me! I forget sometimes how unconnected these sorts of places are. But perhaps Stef can introduce me.'

4

The orphans' heads turned as one to Stef. They could have laid a rasher of bacon on his cheeks and it would be sizzling in seconds. 'B-Benadrylla C-Crumplepatch,' he managed. 'We, we, er, we met the other day. In the, in the, in the . . . pharmacy.'

Cuthbert gasped. 'Ahh! Crumplepatch Industries! You're building the railway. Yes, I'm aware of your businesses. I studied your public accounts a while back, when they were published, in case there were any irregularities. I didn't find any.'

Benadrylla was momentarily taken aback, and Tig added quickly, 'Don't worry. He likes doing that sort of thing. Finds it interesting. Nothing personal.'

'I like them jewels,' said Nellie. 'Diamonds, innit?'

Benadrylla's fingers rose to stroke the necklace protectively. 'Er, yes. They are.' She smiled.

'Nice,' Nellie added approvingly. 'You wanna watch out in Sad Sack, though, there's folks who'll nick those, soon as you take 'em off.' Nellie's eyes were roving over the earrings and necklace in a way that suggested she was one of those people.

'Well . . .' Benadrylla said hesitantly. 'You needn't worry. I shall keep my valuables on my person at all times.' She patted her pockets to demonstrate, and then looked down in surprise as her fingers touched something hairy.

Her brows creased. Pamela had the hem of Benadrylla's dress in her mouth and was chewing it with the air of a restaurant critic trying to decide how many stars to give the meal.

'Pammy!' Herc leaped across and wrestled the fabric out of the goat's mouth. There was a ripping sound. 'Naughty!' he scolded Pamela. 'They're not *real* flowers.'

Benadrylla clutched the dress, her knuckles white. She swallowed noisily. 'Never mind,' she said presently, through gritted teeth. 'Only a little tear. What an interesting choice of pet.'

'You're lucky,' Nellie pointed out truthfully. Until recently, if someone came away from Pamela with nothing more than torn clothing, they could count themselves lucky. 'Sometimes she headbutts people. Once, she—'

Ashna coughed loudly and Nellie stopped, glancing at her with concern. Ashna's lungs flared up regularly. 'You all right, Ash? Need a glass of water?'

'Fine,' Ashna said pointedly. 'Sorry. I should have covered my mouth with my hand. Because we can't just *let everything out*, can we?'

The businesswoman seemed not to notice the meaningful looks passing between the orphans, busy as she was taking a step away while trying to keep the goat in her line of sight.

'This is quite *heavy*,' said the boy loudly.

Benadrylla directed him to place the basket on the ground, and they all crowded round as he pulled off the cloth. Inside were jars of all kinds of preserves, a wheel of delicate yellow cheese, rashers of pink bacon, and a bunch of silver cutlery tied in a ribbon. Herc gasped and instantly began rummaging in the basket, throwing the cutlery to one side.

'Herc . . .' Stef hissed. 'Don't just—'

But Benadrylla laid a hand on his arm, gently. 'It's fine,' she said. 'Let the lad enjoy it. Think of it as recognition for all that effort you've put in. It's no easy task to build a place like this, with such rudimentary equipment and no training. I can see you've really done your absolute best, despite all the challenges. Well done you. You deserve it. Tuck in.'

The boy behind her raised an eyebrow, and let out a soft '*Huh!*'

'We're happy to share,' Stef offered, gesturing to him.

But the boy sneered. 'I don't need your charity. I'm a deputy manager for Crumplepatch Railways, not a loser like you.'

Benadrylla shot him an exasperated pout. 'Don't mind Joe, children. He's one of my *grumpier* workers, aren't you? Say sorry.'

71

Joe's jaw muscles worked for a moment, then he said, 'Yes, madam. *Apologies.*'

The children shuffled uncomfortably in the silence that followed, but then Benadrylla broke it. 'You're probably wondering why I'm here. I don't make a habit of turning up at people's *residences* unannounced.' She smiled indulgently.

'You're right, you shouldn't,' Herc put in, his mouth full of sausage roll. 'The last time someone came to our house unexpectedly they ended up de—'

'Desperately late for their next appointment,' said Cuthbert hastily. 'Anyway, do continue. What's the purpose of your visit?'

Benadrylla beamed round at them all. 'Why, I came to offer you all jobs.'

Chapter Nine

If he were honest, Stef had been just a little disappointed when Benadrylla made him a security guard, three weeks ago.

It astonished him how quickly the camp had come together. In Ralph Cornswallop's field, on the other side of the road from the woods where cows had once grazed, a canvas city now sprawled – more than fifty tents, maybe as many as a hundred. Next to those lay all sorts of equipment – long pieces of iron, carts full of coal, strange machinery with vicious teeth that could slice through the metal. And all around it, bustling, sweating workers, lifting, carrying, cutting, fitting, repairing, digging.

Not him, though. Mostly, he had to stand still next to things. Today it was the carthorses, and the stench of their manure rose into the hazy air, slowly baking in the heat. The horses shuffled and champed and blew out their nostrils at him in a friendly sort of way.

He knew why she'd done it. It was because of how he looked. He was used to people clocking his height, and his scar, and assuming he was a fighter, a bruiser, hard as nails. Nellie had laughed when he'd told her, and maintained he was far too nice to scare any potential thieves away. He didn't feel particularly observant, either. He tended to wander around lost in thought, not paying attention to things around him. Back before he and Nellie had known each other she'd picked his pockets with no trouble at all. She could probably have picked his nose if she'd wanted to, except his own finger was usually up there.

Not that there was anything wrong with being a security guard – it just wasn't really *him*. It would be better when his training started. Benadrylla was putting together a programme for him, working on all sorts of different skills – carpentry, plumbing, mechanics – so that he could then choose to specialize in something. And those skills would also be useful for improving Marshmallow. He could construct a bit of raised decking outside his hut, for starters. For the first time in ages, he was actually looking forward to something. He couldn't wait to get started, but Benadrylla had been so busy that she hadn't had time to organize the training yet. So, for now, he was stuck here.

But at least he was part of something exciting, even if the actual work was being done by others. He watched the hundreds of navvies heading off down the road hauling railway sleepers, often not returning, at least not until after he'd clocked off. Everyone else seemed to be doing longer shifts than him, which was odd.

And it wasn't so bad. Nobody showed any inclination to steal the equipment he was guarding, and every now and then the navvies nodded to him as they passed, with a cheery 'All right?' He'd even been able to help out when a man staggered past him holding a sack of sand which had slipped from his grasp. Between them, they had hauled it into place. And then, a short distance down the road where they were building Sad Sack station, the foreman needed a little extra help winching up a steel beam, and Stef had lent his strength to the team pulling on the rope. Every 'Cheers, mate' and 'Nice one' made his heart tingle.

Even Bickley's frequent presence on site wasn't enough to get him down. The pharmacist turned up nearly every day, pestering Benadrylla to introduce him to any important officials that might be around, trying to sell her his remedies, criticizing Stef's posture, the state of his uniform, the way his shoelaces were tied, until Benadrylla had finally snapped and told him to mind his own business. After that, Bickley had confined himself to staring at Stef disapprovingly – it was as though the pharmacist were a yappy pet dog that she could command with a word.

Benadrylla had gone out of her way to make Stef's life easier. She even provided him with a free uniform, whereas all the other workers had had to pay for theirs. Her generosity was a little awkward, especially after his friends had turned her down. She'd offered them all jobs, and permanent places to live for as long as they continued working for Crumplepatch Industries – anywhere they wanted.

The others had not felt any scruple in rejecting all this. Tig and Nellie, especially, reckoned he was being gullible. Nellie said she'd only just escaped a lifetime of having to take orders from other people and wasn't going to start that again.

For Stef, it was more complicated. He had happily accepted the job, but not the chance to live somewhere else. He didn't want to seem ungrateful, but the truth was he didn't want to leave the others, even though they sometimes drove him mad. And once he'd had his training he could make Marshmallow a proper little village, with home comforts. He had to admit there was something special about coming home at the end of the day and sleeping in a bed he'd made himself, under a roof he'd made himself, even if every now and then part of it fell on him in the night.

'Oi, you.'

He was jolted out of his reverie by a shout from behind him. Joe was approaching. Stef lifted his hand in a friendly wave. 'Hey, Joe.'

Joe gave him a quick up-and-down sneer. 'If you're not too busy standing around doing nothing, I've got a job for you.'

'I'm not actually—'

'Good. Loosen the nuts on those cartwheels.' He gestured at a wooden flatbed cart. 'They're worn out, so I need to replace them, but *she's* given me a thousand other things to do this morning. *Some* of us don't get let home early, you know.'

Stef bit his lip. He wasn't sure Joe had any authority to tell him what to do, but he didn't want to be rude. 'Er, well, thing is, I've been told to guard here.'

'And you are. You can do this at the same time. I'll be back with the new nuts later.' He began to walk off.

Stef hurried after him and grabbed his arm. 'Hang on, I'm supposed to—'

Joe looked down pointedly at Stef's hand on his sleeve until Stef withdrew it. 'I'm in charge of this site when Ms Crumplepatch isn't here. She told me you were keen to help and that I should put you to good use. Or do I need to tell her she's wrong? Are you *not* the living saint she's cracked you up to be?'

Stef opened his mouth, but Joe's obvious hostility had stung him into silence. If he wasn't mistaken, the boy was jealous. But why, exactly? Joe clearly had a more senior, trusted position in the company than he did. He was often at Benadrylla's side – or rather, trailing behind her.

Joe sighed. 'There's a wrench in that blue toolbox by the ladder. I take it you know how to use it?'

Stef wanted to say he had practically built the whole of Marshmallow. Of *course* he knew how to use a wrench. But he bit down on his hurt pride and merely nodded.

With Joe gone, a quick check over the cart confirmed the job was nothing very complicated.

It would take no more than ten minutes. And he was still technically guarding the area, so that was OK.

He set to work.

'There you are, reliable as ever.'

Stef blinked and straightened up as Benadrylla came towards him, her blonde hair and diamond necklace almost blinding in the sunlight. Almost two hours later, there was still no sign of Joe, so Stef had returned the wrench to the toolbox and resumed his guarding stance, swaying slightly in the heat.

'I hear such good things about you,' Benadrylla told him, smiling. 'I knew I was right to pick you.'

Stef found he could only half laugh, half shrug. He was not used to compliments.

'I hope Joe has been making you feel welcome,' she added, and Stef's awkwardness intensified. 'He can be . . . prickly. You must let me know if he causes you any trouble. I am quite a tolerant employer, but I won't stand for bullying.' Then Benadrylla's eye caught something in the distance and her face fell. 'Oh . . . dear me.' Stef followed her gaze to where a small man in a grey suit holding a bulging briefcase was trotting towards them, picking his way around a stack of planks. 'What does *he* want?' She took a deep breath and fixed her lips into an upward curve. 'Finnick! How can I help you . . . *this time?*'

The man arrived out of breath, wiping his forehead with an embroidered hanky. 'Goodness me, Ms Crumplepatch, you are a hard lady to find! One moment you were right beside me on the high street and the next . . . *poof!* Gone! Luckily the pharmacist was able to point me in your direction.'

'Yes. How very lucky,' said Benadrylla drily. She turned to Stef. 'This is Mr Finnick, from the Ministry of FUN. He has been sent to observe our work here. In great detail.' Stef detected the faintest of eye-rolls, which passed quickly, as though she might have been merely stretching her eyebrows.

'Yes, yes,' Finnick was saying, poking the hanky in his breast pocket. 'I report to the Head Minister for FUN himself, Stapleford Pinch.'

'Indeed,' said Benadrylla, teasingly. 'We must get everything right, or FUN will lock us up.'

Finnick was taken aback. 'Heavens, no,' he insisted. 'We don't lock anyone up! We would pass you on to DEATH and get them to do it.' He licked his finger and took a paper from his file. 'Now, I must tell you that I have seen *several* violations of health and safety policy . . . I've noticed quite a few sharp objects, hacksaws and the like, lying around in contravention of the Sharp Objects In Public Spaces regulations three to forty-three. They'll need a protective sponge case on when not actually in use.'

'Oh but those aren't tools,' she said. 'They're exhibits.'

'Exhibits?'

'Yes. They're on display. And, as I'm sure you know, exhibitions are exempt from those regulations. I think they brighten up the place no end, don't you agree? Anything else?' She gave him a winning smile.

From just behind Finnick came the *schh-schh-schh* sound of a saw being drawn back and forth across a plank. Finnick made a small movement as though to turn around, and then looked into Benadrylla's eyes and apparently thought better of it.

'Merely on display. I see. Well, if you're sure . . .'

Benadrylla beamed. 'You darling man! Isn't he a darling?' she asked Stef.

Stef felt unqualified to judge, so he simply stood politely.

'Only one more thing.' Finnick licked his lips and took another paper from his case, unfolding a map in front of them. 'I need you to confirm the precise route through Knott Wood.'

Benadrylla waved him away. 'Oh, must we do this now? I think another time—'

'*Through?*'

Both Finnick and Benadrylla turned in surprise, and Stef realized he had rather yelped it. Between their heads he could see that the map showed Sad Sack and Little Wazzock and the green mass of the woods in between. There was an unmistakeable hatched line cutting all the way through Knott Wood.

'But . . . you said you were following the road *around*.' Benadrylla was staring at Stef oddly, so he felt compelled to go on. 'You know. Around the woods. That's what you told us.' He was sure she had said *around*, not *through*. Almost certain.

Finnick perked up, as though Stef had just offered him a plate of explanation sandwiches. If there was one thing FUN officials enjoyed, it was spelling things out unnecessarily. 'Mathematics tells us that the shortest distance between two points is a straight line,' he said.

'We follow the road up to the woods,' Benadrylla added, 'and *then* we go through. You must have misheard me.' Her voice was kind, soft, and maybe just a little bit wary.

He was sure he hadn't misheard. But his friends were always telling him he was 'away with the fairies' half the time.

Oh no.

'But . . . but . . . you said Marshmallow was really good, you said—'

She was gentle, concerned. 'Stef . . . Stef. You weren't expecting to be able to *stay* in your funny little camp?' She read the answer from his stricken face. 'Oh, you poor thing. What a horrible misunderstanding. Don't get me wrong, your handiwork is marvellous – considering it's the work of children. It's *adorable*. And you've been having such a fun adventure! Such an *educational* experience. But it's not . . . real, is it now? Surely you knew that. Why did you think I offered you and your friends a place to stay, as well as work? It's obvious you can't play in there for ever.' She laughed, a tinkling sound that crushed his heart and told him he was the most foolish boy alive. 'You've had a lovely game, and now it's time to move out.'

Stef's breath was coming fast, and his throat wasn't working properly; he swallowed convulsively. Marshmallow was no game, but in the face of her laughter he suddenly couldn't explain it. He cast around for reasons. 'But . . . I mean . . . you'll have to chop trees down.'

Benadrylla nodded sympathetically. 'I applaud your environmental concern. But we simply cannot go around. There's a spring in the middle of the woods, and we must have a water stop there. Steam trains aren't much good without water, are they?'

And as he watched in horror, she traced the line through Marshmallow on the map with her sharp, manicured fingernail.

Sad
Sack

Cornswallop
Farm

Crumplepatch
Railways

Lardidar Valley

Little Wazzock

St Halibut's
Home for Waifs
and Strays

'**W**hat do you mean, she's NICE?' Tig had said, when Stef had dropped his bombshell to them all. 'She wants to destroy our home! How can she be *nice*?'

They were gathered around the main firepit.

'It was a misunderstanding,' Stef said wretchedly. 'She thought we knew. She didn't realize we meant to stay.'

Tig looked sideways at him. 'Come *on*. She's obviously been stringing you along. Probably hoped you'd feel so grateful for the job that you'd cave in and persuade us all to move out.'

Cuthbert raised an eyebrow thoughtfully. 'Indeed. She knew we were in her way but, legally, she can't lay a hand on us so she needs us to go voluntarily. Oh, clever!'

Stef shook his head. Benadrylla was not the manipulative villain they were making out. He felt suddenly out on a limb. No one seemed to care that his job was at stake here.

'Yeah, this way we wouldn't give her no trouble,' Nellie put in. 'Ooh, *love* your little camp, so *quirky*, so *adorable*!' She mimicked Benadrylla's honeyed tones. 'If she thinks she's building through Marshmallow she's got another think coming. We've got that legal-loophole fingy – right, Cuth? We ain't going nowhere. This place is the bee's knees.' Nellie had been moaning only that morning that there was an ants' nest under her hut. But her complaints had dried up the moment there was the prospect of a fight. 'I'll lie in front of the tracks, if I 'ave to.'

'We might have to do that,' Ashna said grimly. 'We're sort-of-allowed to be here, but so is she. The only thing she can't do is hurt us.'

'And she doesn't want to do that anyway,' added Stef firmly. 'You don't need to make her out to be a monster. It's just . . . unlucky that she planned the route here.' As he said it, though, he imagined their huts being knocked down so that the tracks could be laid. He felt his heart flip. He didn't want to lose Marshmallow any more than they did. But he didn't want a fight with Benadrylla, either. She was his only chance to do something useful, learn new things, bring some purpose to his life. There had to be a way to resolve this amicably.

'You are on *our* side, right?' Tig muttered.

Stef's cheeks flamed. How could she think he wasn't?

Herc came to his rescue. 'Of course he's on our side!' But he raised a questioning eyebrow at Stef to confirm, which made Stef's stomach turn over with sudden loneliness. Did even Herc doubt him now? Pamela was giving him one of her unsettling stares, her jaw halted mid-chew on a chamomile flower, as though awaiting his response. He stared back at her defiantly, and she tossed her horns lightly and went back to chewing. Not long ago she'd have headbutted him halfway across the clearing for daring to catch her eye.

'We could take her to court,' Cuthbert suggested. 'Tie her up in a legal case for ages. I mean, she'd probably win in the end, but it would buy us time.'

'Perhaps we could get a petition going instead,' pondered Tig. 'Sad Sackers get cross about much sillier things.'

Ashna shook her head. 'Bickley thinks it's the dawning of a great new age for Sad Sack – he's hanging around that Crumplepatch woman like a bad smell, trying to offer her advice the whole time. And he's hoping the railway will bring more people to the whole area, so he can flog them more rubbish. No one's going to put their name on a petition against something he wants. Everyone in Sad Sack is loopy for him these days – they think he's some kind of wizard.'

'More people?' Tig scoffed. 'He hates people. He doesn't even like the ones that are already here.'

'Arfur will be on our side,' Herc pointed out. 'And Maisie. And Ma Yeasty.'

But Cuthbert shook his head. 'It doesn't make any difference. They can't do anything about it. They're just citizens, like us. They have no power. Arfur's already adopted us – if he gets involved it'll just draw attention to the fact that he's not actually here taking care of us. That's not a fact we really want DEATH or FUN to be thinking about right now.'

'Sabotage,' said Nellie quietly, narrowing her eyes. 'It's the only way.'

'I know,' piped up Herc. 'We could explode her equipment!'

'Whoa, whoa, stop! You're all getting carried away.' Stef bit his lip.

'And you're just thinking of yourself,' Tig snapped back. 'So you've got a nice cushy job – is that more important to you than we are?'

Stef was stung. So he was worried about losing his job – what was wrong with that? He could equally turn it around: why didn't *they* worry about it, since it was important to *him*? Especially Tig. She'd always looked out for him; now his feelings were irrelevant, apparently. But he bit back the retort. It would just make the argument worse.

'What you're talking about doing would just upset her, ruin everything, *and* break the law in a serious way. You can't just destroy someone's property.' He considered for a second. They had, technically, done that before. 'I mean, you *shouldn't*, not on purpose. It's morally wrong. Let me talk to her,' he added. 'I reckon I can persuade her not to go through the woods after all. She's a businesswoman. If I give her good business reasons, she'll listen.'

He'd tried to think of it from Benadrylla's point of view. There were real benefits to laying the tracks around the forest, next to the road. For a start, cutting down trees was intensive, hard work – the ground by the road was wide, and flat; they could lay tracks in half, maybe a quarter, of the time it would take to hack their way through the woods, even if they had to lay more of them. The thing she'd said about needing water . . . Well, why not fill up the trains at Sad Sack instead?

It was just plain business sense. Probably.

'I'll talk to her tomorrow. In the meantime . . . just . . . relax, OK? Don't . . . *do* anything.' If he did this right, he could keep his job, they could keep Marshmallow, and everyone would be happy.

With great reluctance, the others agreed, and Stef went

90

to bed early, exhausted but hopeful. As he walked to his hut, Tig's low mutter carried across the clearing, and her contemptuous tone was a stab to his heart.

'What a waste of time.'

The others were wakeful late into the night, sitting around the fire toasting Herc's marshmallows (still a little chewy, in Tig's opinion).

Nellie was adamant. 'I ain't sitting here and waiting while them tracks is coming closer. Stef is never gonna be able to persuade her. We should prepare, like. For war. No shots fired yet, but at least load the musket, type of thing.'

Cuthbert frowned at her. 'Why do you have to use such violent imagery? It's *information* we need.'

Tig nodded. 'I guess I could go check out Little Wazzock, see if they've started at that end yet. Maybe we could slow her down, somehow.'

'I might go to Powders 'n' Potions.' Ashna had her head in her chin, staring off into the trees towards Sad Sack.

'What? Why?' Tig asked.

Ashna frowned distractedly. 'I don't know. I just think Bickley is up to something. I mean, up to something more than he usually is. I don't like it. Maybe it's connected to Benadrylla's railway.'

'Give over,' Nellie told her, with a good-natured dig to the ribs. 'I ain't no fan of Benadrylla, but she won't even give Bickley the time of day no matter how much he tries to suck up to her.'

'You're all missing the point,' Cuthbert said. 'We don't even know how long we've got. What we need is Benadrylla's *schedule*. I bet that man from FUN has the papers in that briefcase Stef says he carries everywhere.'

Nellie's head jerked up. 'All right, now we're talking. Tomorrow, we'll borrow that briefcase.'

Tig nodded. 'OK. But look, let's not tell Stef about any of this. I get the feeling he wouldn't approve.'

'Hey, Nellie.' Herc tugged her sleeve. 'Can I go with you and Cuthbert?'

Nellie laughed. 'Yeah, sure – let's bring a brass band an' all, that always helps with sneakin' around.'

Herc frowned uncertainly. 'Really? I don't think it would.'

'Please say no,' Tig told Nellie, 'or he'll go and find a pair of cymbals and a trumpet.'

Nellie considered for a moment. 'Tell you what, Herc, I'll bring you back a prezzie, all right? Something from the camp, to play with?'

'No one *ever* lets me join in.'

Tig turned to Herc and saw his eyes were shining, his

92

lip jutting. Perhaps she should include him somehow. Besides, if he stayed here alone, he was sure to make a mess or break something. She laid a hand on his shoulder.

'I have a very special and important job for you, little brother.'

✨ *Chapter Eleven* ✨

The following morning, even before the crow had cleared its throat, Stef got up to make his way to the camp. During the walk, light began to filter across the sky and he could already hear the sounds of activity and see row upon row of white tents, their sides rippling in the breeze. There was movement all over it, as workers scurried between tasks. Navvies were hauling equipment across the road to the trees, and a group of lumberjacks gathered around the start of the path that led to Marshmallow, axes gleaming at their sides. Benadrylla was right: they weren't wasting any time – he had to act fast.

As he approached the outskirts of the camp, he passed a train engine on top of a set of blocks, two pairs of oil-stained trousers poking out below, their owners doing something to its underside. His eyes roved over the engine as he passed, taking in its glossy, polished green body. A large chimney stood proudly at the front, rivets dotting its surface. Inside he knew there would be a boiler, and a place for someone to stand and feed coals in. It was a miracle of engineering – the very best money could buy. Yesterday he would have felt a squirm of excitement in his belly; today the sight of it just made him feel nauseous.

Hissing and clanking filled the air as a huge, steam-powered excavator was tested, black smoke pouring from a chimney at its rear. Workers gathered around it to watch as a woman with a clipboard gestured and shouted to be heard over the din, directing the driver this way and that.

Stef was walking into a camp full of hundreds of lumberjacks and track engineers and joiners, about to ask the head of a hugely successful company to change the course of a railroad.

Benadrylla's office was the largest tent in the camp. Stef approached the closed canvas flap and hesitated, then knocked on the fabric and immediately felt foolish when it made no sound. He could hear her berating someone inside; whoever it was seemed not to be responding, which made her even more irate. He had not heard her shout like that before – she was always so measured and kind; it was unnerving.

'If you don't shape up, you'll be out, do you hear? You're an embarrassment. Stop snivelling. You can't follow a simple order without messing it up—'

Stef jumped as the flap was suddenly flung back and Benadrylla emerged, startling at his presence and closing the canvas swiftly behind her.

'Stef!' she said, and her voice was like honey once

more. She must have clocked his expression because she added, 'I have to tell my employees off every now and then. I hate doing it. But sometimes people try to take advantage. Gosh, you look very hot and thirsty. Here, have a cool drink.' She popped back inside and emerged a few moments later with a glass of milk. He took a grateful sip. 'Everything all right?'

He took a breath to steady his nerves. 'Yes. Thank you. I just wanted to talk to you about something. Give you a suggestion, in fact.'

She smiled. 'Wonderful. Do you know, I *love* that in an employee. You're not just someone who sits around and has to be nagged to do any work, are you? Not like *some* people around here. You have ideas. Spark. Intelligence.' She was speaking very loudly, as though he were hard of hearing. A couple of lumberjacks nearby nudged each other, giggled, and pointed.

'Do you know, if I had a son, I'd want him to be just like you. Brave and strong.'

A rush of air left him in a laugh. He'd worked hard, for sure, but it was a ridiculous, outrageous compliment to someone she barely knew.

'Now, I would love to hear your idea, but I have a few things to do first.' She gestured back into the tent, with a sigh. 'Tell you what: there's always something to

97

fix in a place like this. You're probably bored of guarding things, aren't you?' He gave a half-nod, half-headshake, accompanied by an awkward little noise like a puppy whining. 'I think the steam excavator needs some attention, for a start. Why don't you see if you can help out around the place, and I'll come and find you later for a chat?'

He nodded. The more he impressed her with his willingness to work, the more likely she'd be to listen to his idea.

The operator of the steam excavator seemed to be on a break, so he took the chance to admire the great machine, running his hands over the steel, marvelling at the strength and size of it. It wasn't hard to see how it worked, at least on a basic level. Water was held in a large tank, and heated in a coal furnace housed at the rear – the black smoke he'd seen earlier coming from the chimney. The steam was forced through pipes and powered the engine, enabling all the moving parts to work. Running a finger over the gigantic steel teeth of the shovel at the front, he shivered involuntarily. Such a machine would make light work of their huts.

'Hey, get away from there.' Stef turned to see Joe striding towards him, and his heart sank. As always, the boy was scowling. 'What're you up to?'

'Benadrylla said I should help out.'

The boy's eyebrows shot up. 'On first-name terms, are we? Best of friends with the boss? Must be nice.' He eyed Stef's glass. 'Well, when you've had your little *ice-cold drinkie*, the excavator tank's dry. See if you can manage to fill it from that.' The boy pointed to a large barrel nearby, with a jug on top. 'That's about your level, I reckon.'

Stef refused to rise to the bait. He drained the glass, set it down and simply said, 'All right. I will.' He dipped the jug into the murky water and poured it into the tank while the boy hopped up to the cab and adjusted something inside. 'Did you get those cartwheels sorted OK yesterday?' he tried, hoping to wear Joe down with relentless cheery chat.

The only reply was an affirmative grunt.

'This water's not very clean,' Stef called up.

'Yeah. Sad Sack's finest. This place is such a dump.'

Stef swallowed his pride. He'd lived in Sad Sack almost all his life. Even if, objectively speaking, it really was a dump, it was rude to point it out. Instead he said, 'Seems it's good enough for Ms Crumplepatch.'

The boy laughed, a harsh exclamation. 'You daft or something? She's barely here.' He glanced down. 'Got a nice room at the Palatial Hotel. Hot running water, room service, clean towels. Spent most of the day yesterday shopping. You won't catch her roughing it out here with the rest of us more than she has to.'

The boy's tone was scathing and Stef felt defensive on Benadrylla's behalf. She was the boss, after all. Why shouldn't she enjoy a few luxuries? 'She seems nice,' he replied mildly.

The boy gave a loud guffaw, then leaned down. 'Nice? Don't you have eyes? Look around you. See anyone else getting a cold drink while they're on shift?'

Stef didn't know how to respond. He found most of the other workers a bit intimidating – a sweaty mass of muscle and dust. But now the boy had mentioned it, the discrepancy was obvious. To his left, he saw a cart full of workers being driven out on to the road; they were practically heaped on top of each other, faces smeared with grime, flopping with exhaustion, barely able to sit up. The hairs on his neck prickled. Benadrylla gave him a shiny coin at the end of every day, but now he thought about it, he hadn't seen anyone else getting paid. His gut twisted anxiously. Something wasn't right. He was starting to wonder if he was being fobbed off. But he couldn't exactly admit that to Joe. 'Well, it's because I'm new, I expect. A trainee.'

Joe laughed, an unpleasant, hard sound. 'Training. *Right.* Hah!'

Stef bristled. 'Actually, she has plans to develop my career.'

This only made the boy laugh harder. 'Yeah, she's got plans for you, all right. You and your woodland pals.'

'Right.' Stef slammed the lid of the tank shut, his patience suddenly run dry. 'Is there something you want to say to me?'

Joe jumped down from the cab and fixed Stef with a glare of such anguished hostility that Stef took a step back. 'I've got *nothing* to say to you. Just stay away from me.'

✎ Chapter Twelve ✎

shna's mind was entirely elsewhere when she walked straight into Ralph Cornswallop on her way down the high street. The first she noticed of his presence was when she got a faceful of tweed and a whiff of farmyard.

'No barging in, lass. Get to the back of the line.'

Ashna looked, and indeed there was a line of a dozen or so people behind him, stretching up to the closed door of Powders 'n' Potions. To her surprise, Ma Yeasty and Sue Perglue were both there, too, presumably leaving their shops unattended. Sue Perglue was humming a vaguely familiar tune. What was going on?

Ashna mumbled an apology to Cornswallop, and he went back to peering eagerly through the door, his nose squashed up against the glass.

'Everything OK, Ma Yeasty?' she asked cautiously.

Ma Yeasty swatted at one of the flies that followed her

everywhere she went, attracted by the three-month-old syrup stains on her apron. 'Right as rain, my love! Right as rain! We're all aflutter – Mr Brimstone has performed his best miracle yet.'

Ashna raised one eyebrow half an inch. 'What's he done?'

Ma Yeasty leaned towards her, eyes round and glittering. 'He's brought Betty back from the dead!' Betty was Ralph Cornswallop's wife, who had run the farm with him.

Ralph Cornswallop peeled his nose off the door just long enough to nod enthusiastically. 'Turned up this morning, fresh as a daisy! I couldn't believe me eyes. So happy I was, shouting, "It's a miracle! You're alive!" and she looks me lovingly right in the eye, and says, "Will yer shut yer face about ruddy miracles and take a bath – you stink." Oh, it were like she'd never died! And it's Bickley Brimstone and his tea I have to thank for it.'

Ashna could not hold back a guffaw. 'That's . . . just not possible. Come *on*.'

'I'm coming back every day from now on,' said Ma Yeasty, as though Ashna had not spoken. 'There isn't a problem he can't fix.'

Sue cut in. 'Third time this week for me. I suffer from stress, see, and I come out of that back room feeling like

103

I've had a full night's sleep, he's that good.'

Ma Yeasty made noises of agreement, and the whole line nodded together like a badly synchronized dance troupe. 'Maisie's just had an "energy rebalancing" session. She was bone-tired when she went in, the labour of taking care of all them kiddies, I expect. Came out all perky, didn't she, Sue? Like a new woman.'

Ashna could hardly believe it. The pharmacist must be making a packet from all this.

'What exactly happens in there? How does it work?'

But at this there was silence. Then Ma Yeasty tapped her head. 'He can do *anything*. It's beyond our understanding, love.'

Ashna walked off in a daze. It was certainly beyond hers. It sounded very much as though Bickley was making it up as he went along. All she was sure of was that he was up to no good; she needed to talk through her suspicions with someone, but everyone back at Marshmallow was focused only on Benadrylla.

Her feet seemed to take her of their own accord down the alley between St Cod's and the Mending House. In this crazy world, a con man was probably the only person they could trust. Arfur couldn't stand Bickley Brimstone, and was too streetwise to fall into whatever had made such fools of the other Sad Sackers. One con man will always see through another. Besides that, he had connections; perhaps he could do some digging on Benadrylla.

In the alley she could immediately see evidence of Arfur's pigeons. One or two were perched on the guttering around the Mending House roof, cooing softly. The alley was spattered with their droppings, and a feather or two lay on the cobbles.

Arfur had constructed a coop for the pigeons, a lean-to against the back of the Mending House. It was ten feet long, made from wooden struts and chicken wire, with steel buckets lying on their sides on shelves at the back for the pigeons to nest in. He kept his library cart, which doubled as his bed, next to it. The cart had once been used to carry the post, hitched to Maisie's trusty pony Bernard. It was a simple affair, with a curved roof, small windows at the sides, and a door which opened at the back to form a ramp to the ground. There was a place for the driver to sit out front, separated from the inside of the cart by a piece of canvas that formed a curtain.

Maisie had given permission for this set-up on the basis that she could keep an eye on Arfur and would immediately be able to tell if he started using the place to handle stolen goods, or anything else too dodgy. Officially, his address was the Mending House itself, but Maisie had made it clear she would rather live with a rabid, flea-ridden fox than with Arfur. She'd tried it once, even marrying him, and had declared it the biggest mistake she'd ever made.

As Ashna approached, she could hear Maisie's voice.

'I can't believe you won't even try it, Arfur,' she was saying. 'You spend too much time with those stupid pigeons. You need more intelligent company.'

'Oi! They ain't stupid. They're homing pigeons.' Arfur was being selective with the truth, here. They had indeed been bred as homing pigeons, but were rejects, which was why he had acquired them for free. Their greatest skill, apart from annoying Bickley, was accidentally flying into brick walls, and they never went further afield than Sad Sack. Nevertheless, Arfur would accept no criticism of them.

'Pah!' Maisie laughed. 'Those things couldn't find their way home if you put them in a taxicab and rolled out a red carpet to the door.'

There was a moment's hurt silence, then Arfur said, 'That ain't true. We got a connection, me and these birds. They got love in their hearts. Unlike some.'

Maisie let out an exasperated sigh, stomped round the corner in a strop and narrowly avoided barrelling into Ashna. ''Scuse me,' she said crossly. 'Ooooh, that man!'

Ashna watched her go in surprise. As Maisie neared the end of the alley she began to hum the familiar six-note ditty Ashna had heard from Ma Yeasty and Sue Perglue. Now she recognized it – the pharmacist's clock chime. Her anxiety increased.

Arfur was wiping down the shelves inside the coop. He seemed to take far more care of the pigeons than he did of himself. They were well fed, their feathers glossy, their bodies plump – whereas he himself resembled a grubby shirt

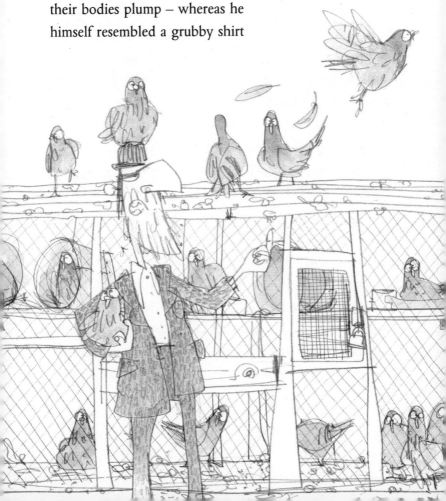

and trousers on a greasy coat-hanger.

'All right, Ash,' he greeted her. 'How's tricks in the woods?'

'Arfur,' she said. 'Why is Maisie such a fan of Bickley all of a sudden?'

He shrugged and continued to wipe, stopping only to give a small grey pigeon an affectionate stroke with the cloth. 'Guess he's won her round with his charms.' He winked at her.

'I'm serious. There's something fishy going on. I don't know what he's telling them all in there but he's fooling them somehow, to make money. Maybe something more sinister, too. I don't like it – they can't even remember what he's said to them, but they think he's some sort of miracle worker.'

Arfur shrugged again, infuriatingly. 'Can't save people from themselves if they want to be pillocks.'

She decided to come right out and say it. 'I think he's hypnotizing people, Arfur. The way they all go on about how relaxing the sessions are, and they've all started humming that weird little tune from his clock. I thought it was getting a bit much during the fair, but now it's way out of hand. He's convinced them he's brought Betty Cornswallop back from the dead! That tea must do something to their brains, soften them up or something so that he can hypnotize them.'

Arfur gave a head rub to the closest pigeon and it closed its eyes in bliss. 'He don't have the wits for that. But y'know, wouldn't be so bad if he *is* hypnotizing them. Can't make 'em any more annoying than they already are, can he?' He chuckled.

'You don't think *anything* is your problem, do you? What if Bickley uses his tricks to help Benadrylla Crumplepatch get rid of us? She's trying to lay tracks through Marshmallow and you couldn't care less.'

'Come on, that ain't fair. You'll be OK, won't ya? What about your legal-loophole fingy?'

'You've left us all alone out there—'

'Now hang on just one flamin' minute, that's exactly what you wanted—'

'I'm *sure* Bickley Brimstone is involved with that railway somehow. And now Maisie's joined his fan club! How could you be so unfeeling, *Dad*?'

Arfur sucked in his teeth, and appealed to his pigeons. 'You 'ear that? You 'ear what she just said?' His pigeons cooed and bobbed their heads in sympathy. He turned back to her. 'And what exactly am I supposed to do about it?'

Ah, there it was, finally. She tried not to smile, but couldn't help it.

'Thought you'd never ask.'

People tended to walk away from Finnick. He didn't take it personally. Everyone was so busy these days, and it was rare to find anyone who had time to discuss the subjects that truly fascinated him, like document formatting.

So when the boy approached him at the small table he had set up to work on at the edge of the camp and struck up a conversation on kerning, he was happy to help. Most people didn't even know what kerning was. It was a mystery how they got through life. But he and this very well-spoken child had been discussing the matter now for a good ten minutes. He had been feeling inexplicably low, and this had cheered him right up.

'May I ask you,' he said to the boy, 'your name, and what your role is here? I have never met anyone outside of FUN who shares my interest in the noble art of spacing words correctly. Ms Crumplepatch thought kerning was some kind of sport involving sliding around on ice.'

The boy waved a hand dismissively. 'Oh, I'm Cuthbert. I'm a freelance consultant managing administrative assistant directing supervisor. Just here for the day.' There was a loud bird call from the woods, and the boy seemed to remember something. 'Is that the time?' he said, looking nowhere in particular. 'Lovely to meet you.' Then he was off.

Finnick watched him sadly as he melted into the trees. Perhaps they'd bump into each other again and have another jolly good chat. He seemed like the sort of fellow who might have strong opinions on filing.

Talking of which, there was still some alphabetization cross-checking to do.

Finnick reached for his briefcase under the table.

It wasn't there.

Herc was beginning to wonder if his sister would ever trust him.

He'd *known* the special and important job would turn out to be something stupid. 'Go and buy some hay for Pamela,' she'd said. 'She keeps chewing the rubber off my roof.'

It was so unfair. It wasn't as if he hadn't already proved himself. He had, just a few months ago, single-handedly saved them all from the wicked villain Ainderby Myers, using his skill with explosives. After that, he'd thought they'd all stop treating him like a baby. But no – if anything, Tig was even less keen for him to do his science experiments, even though they were completely educational and had only once actually injured someone. OK, twice. Three times if you counted a few teensy stitches.

He sighed, kicking at the grass as he made his way back across the fields with the hay he'd bought from the farmhouse. There had been no sign of any Cornswallop, no answer to his knock, so he'd left the money under a stone and helped himself to a bale. The Cornswallops' fields stretched for a few dozen acres across the top of the ridge opposite Knott Wood, and sloped gently down to the road. The cows normally grazed freely all over, but due to the Crumplepatch Railways takeover of the bottom field, they were fenced in up here instead, shambling about and mooing plaintively, cross at being kept away from the grasses below.

'Tell me about it,' he told them. 'You think you have it bad. At least you're allowed to eat things that've been on the floor.'

A young brown cow trotted up to him and nudged him shyly in the chest. He patted the bridge of her nose and she gave a gentle, sympathetic snort into his palm.

Animals always understood – Pamela, especially, but any animal was a better listener than his sister.

The cow stretched out her neck and began to nibble at the hay.

'Nooo!' Herc said, snatching it away. 'That's Pamela's. You can't have it.'

The cow ducked away, startled at his sudden movement.

'It's all right.' He felt sorry for the nervous young creature and rootled around in his pocket, where he kept everything of value, pulling out a couple of squashed marshmallows. They were a very pale pink – he'd tried adding strawberry flavour, and was pretty pleased with them. 'Here. Try these.'

The cow snaffled them eagerly from his palm with every appearance of enjoyment. Then her eyes grew wide.

'Yeah. I know,' Herc said modestly. 'Not half bad, eh?'

Her hooves skittered on the ground, and she lurched excitedly sideways like a crab. Herc giggled. Then she barrelled into a neighbouring cow, who objected with a loud moo. Other bovine heads looked up from grazing to see the first cow begin galloping in circles, first small ones, then larger ones.

'Steady on,' Herc told her. But she took no notice, scampering around the field like a puppy. The other cows didn't have a clue what was up with their colleague, so they did what they normally did when one of them did something unusual: they copied her. They began to respond, bouncing away and bumping into each other, mooing eagerly, chasing tails and butterflies, gathering speed, at first in no particular direction, just a chaotic ramble – but then they all seemed to get the same idea at once.

'Er . . .' said Herc. The entire herd was galloping towards the slope.

It was OK, though, because the way down was blocked off by a very sturdy new fence. The only way through was the double gate, which was closed.

Herc knew it was, because he'd come through it on the way up.

He was a hundred per cent certain he'd shut it behind him.

Or definitely at least ninety-nine per cent certain.

✤ Chapter Fourteen ✤

'Stef!' came Benadrylla's warm tones. 'So. Did you find much to get on with about the place?'

This was his final chance to impress, and suddenly it didn't feel like he'd done much. He racked his brains. He told her about filling the excavator tank and dredged up all the other small tasks he could remember doing. When he got to telling her that he'd tidied a pile of shovels, he realized that perhaps he should stop talking. She seemed pleased, but slightly confused, when he pointed out the cart Joe had asked him to work on the previous day. He didn't mention Joe, though. Why should Joe get any credit for it?

'This one?' she said in surprise. 'It's brand new. I didn't even know there was anything wrong with it.' She patted the flatbed of the cart. 'You're a marvel. Now, what did you want to discuss?'

Taking a steadying breath, Stef launched into his

prepared speech, about how taking the track *around* the woods made far more sense. He was nervous and stumbled over his words, but on the whole, when he finished, he felt he'd actually been quite persuasive.

To his relief, she smiled. But then she said, 'I understand that you are trying to keep things as they are. But life cannot stand still. The answer is no. I'm sorry.' She reached out and gave him a consoling tap on the arm. 'My offer of accommodation and work to you all still stands – I suggest you take it.'

He swallowed. 'We just can't. I mean, I'd love to keep working for you – and I'm really looking forward to the training – but the others aren't interested. And we have to be in Marshmallow. Knott Wood is the only place we can stay together, and we're really proud of what we've made. Please think again.'

Her next words had lost all warmth, and the smile was gone. 'I had hoped for more gratitude. Bickley Brimstone told me you were afraid of DEATH.' Her eyes narrowed. 'I assure you, there are worse fates than that.'

The blood drained from Stef's head and the scenery seemed to wobble.

She tilted her head to one side. 'I prefer to do things the easy way, where possible. Quietly. Cheaply. With minimum paperwork. But if one of us must be unhappy, it won't be me.' The smile was back, but it wasn't a nice one this time. 'Bickley said I shouldn't have you anywhere near my camp. He said that you and your companions are lying, thieving toerags, and that you'd try to sabotage the work. He said you had a history of damaging other people's property.' She laughed at Stef's shocked expression. 'Oh yes, we had *quite* the chat before you woke up after your accident. I told him I would handle it my way.'

It seemed that Benadrylla had not been quite as intolerant of the pharmacist as she had made out. A ghastly thought slithered into Stef's brain. 'You didn't hire me because you were impressed that I stopped your runaway cab . . . You thought I would persuade my friends to get out of Knott Wood if you were nice to me. You were using me.' The others had told him, and he'd ignored them.

'Take the offer.' Stef startled as she slammed her hand down hard on the cart.

There was an ominous creak, and a soft *plink* from a wheel. Then another.

Stef was relieved to spot Finnick bustling up to them, a welcome distraction. The man from FUN was hugging his briefcase fiercely, like a bear with a pot of honey.

Finnick appeared exhausted. 'Yet again, madam, I have been running around trying to find you. It's almost as though you are avoiding me! Oh, I've had such a day. I

couldn't find my briefcase for a full half an hour, until that nice young freelance consultant person found me again and pointed out it was just where I'd left it. I must be overtired.' He drew a hanky across his perspiring forehead, and leaned against the cart.

One minute they were both there, man and vehicle, and the next there was a tremendous crashing noise, and a cloud of dust. It eventually thinned to reveal Finnick sitting dazedly atop what was effectively a pile of splinters.

With perfect timing, Joe arrived. 'What on earth has happened to that cart?' His eyes slid sideways, and all at once Stef knew he'd been set up.

At first he thought the shuddering was his own fear. But then he heard a deep rumbling and realized the ground underneath them was shaking.

Around them, lumberjacks, navvies, mechanics and drivers paused in their work. Finnick clambered up from the wreckage of the cart in alarm.

A shout came from the edge of the camp, where the flat of the field became a steep slope leading up to the rest of

Cornswallop Farm. People began to point up at the brow of the hill.

Like the first view of a terrible army arriving at a battle, a row of cows had appeared at the very top. Behind them another row, then another, hundreds of them, surging down the slope towards the camp, unstoppable as a tidal wave.

There was an endless stream of them, mooing, galloping, changing direction and barging into each other as though they weren't sure where they were going but had to get there fast.

Finnick raised a slightly trembling finger. 'Ah, you need a licence to keep cattle, madam. You, ah, you need to prevent them from entering the workplace. Here –' He whipped out another form from his briefcase. Benadrylla dashed it from his grasp and it blew away across the field.

'Those aren't mine, you great lummox!'

The first cow reached the edge of the camp, headed straight for a tent, then skidded in the mud and ran around it. The second, third and fourth cows weren't so lucky, and ploughed straight into it, then onwards, dragging a tangled mess of tent poles, canvas and sleeping bags with them.

Finnick's finger was still pointing, pointlessly. 'They are not allowed, not allowed . . .'

But nobody could hear him over the baying of the cows, and the panicked shouts of the lumberjacks and navvies as they scattered before the increasingly terrified animals. The herd continued to pour into the camp through the gate, relentless. There was a crash as several charged into one of the full carts, and it tumbled over, spilling coal to the grass. Stef dragged Finnick and Joe to duck behind a cluster of large barrels.

Finnick gestured to Benadrylla to join them. 'Madam! Take cover! You will be trampled!'

But Benadrylla did not move. She was watching in impotent fury as around her tents collapsed, fabric ripped, horses bolted and pulled their carts in all directions, navvies leaping from the drivers' seats and sprinting for cover. She stood in the midst of it, her skin white

with rage, somehow unscathed, as cows streamed past her on all sides, wild-eyed and snorting.

Many minutes later, there was an eerie silence across the camp. Here and there a cow wandered drunkenly about, but most of them had scattered up the road. Benadrylla was the only thing still upright, like a lone flagpole stuck in the grass. Workers began to crawl stiffly and cautiously from their hiding places underneath upturned carts, trying to disentangle themselves from swathes of tent fabric. The mules and horses were nowhere to be seen.

'Check the equipment,' Benadrylla barked at a nearby navvy. 'I want a report on the damage. NOW.'

Finnick picked his way carefully around the scattered broken planks that had once been the cart, slipping slightly on the mud churned up by the cows. 'Dear me, dear me,' he was saying to himself repeatedly, picking up sodden papers from the ground where he had dropped them in his fright. 'Dear me. I shall need to order a whole new set of forms. What a terrible accident!'

They stood contemplating the scene. Joe picked up a broken axle from the cart pile and pointed it at Stef. 'It's no accident. I *knew* he was up to something, Ms Crumplepatch. Look at this, for a start – he must've loosened the wheel nuts.'

Stef's jaw fell. 'You *told* me to, yesterday!'

Benadrylla narrowed her eyes. 'That seems unlikely.' A smirk appeared on Joe's face, but quickly disappeared at her next words. 'However, Joe, you were supposed to be keeping an eye on him. I'll deal with you later.'

Joe flinched, as though he'd thrown a punch only to find it landed on his own nose.

She approached Stef and began to walk around him, circling slowly. 'The cart and the cows? Am I seeing a pattern? Did you *sabotage* my camp, boy?'

'No!' he cried in horror. 'I told the others we shouldn't!'

That didn't sound as convincing a defence as he'd hoped. 'I've no idea how the cows got in here. That definitely wasn't us. I didn't do anything . . . on purpose, I mean. I just—'

At that moment, an incredulous shout came from a few yards away, next to the excavator. A grimy-overalled woman, who'd been trying and failing to restart it, had opened the cover of the excavator's water tank and was peering inside.

'What flamin' pillock's gone and put *beer* in my tank?'

❧ Chapter Fifteen ❧

erc was running back towards Marshmallow when he heard something coming fast, through the trees.

He'd reckoned, if he got home quick enough, Tig and the others wouldn't suspect him of having anything to do with the cow thing. The key would be to stop just outside the clearing and then saunter in casually with the hay. Cool as a cucumber.

There was a gruff shout some distance behind him and thumping footfalls approached, louder than his own. Instinctively he skidded round a tree trunk, dropped the hay and climbed the side facing away from whoever was coming, planting his toes on a thick branch for support.

From his elevated position, he saw it was not one, but two people: a large man chasing a boy. A few seconds later, they were almost underneath him. The man was carrying a horsewhip, yelling, 'You better run, wimp!' At that moment, the boy's foot caught on a tree root and he

124

fell, sprawling. Herc could hear the breath knocked out of him. The boy's legs scrabbled madly to get up, but the man's foot slammed down on the back of his knee and he yelped in pain. Luckily, neither of them appeared to have noticed the bale of hay that Herc had left at the base of the tree. 'She says I have to give you some nice cuts and bruises,' the man said, rubbing his hands and spitting on them to better hold the whip. 'Always happy to oblige Ms Crumplepatch.'

The boy had turned on to his back and struggled under his pursuer, eyes wide and terrified. Then his gaze passed over the man's shoulder and appeared to spot Herc above him. His brows creased in surprise.

Herc turned his head this way and that; could he find something to throw to the boy as a weapon? A loose branch, maybe?

As if in answer, there came a sharp crack from the one he was standing on.

Tig was worried about Herc. She couldn't help it. It was incredibly inconvenient, because she already had a full-time job worrying about losing their home again, but Herc *still* wasn't back from the farm, and when she didn't know where he was, it usually meant he was somewhere he shouldn't be.

Stef wasn't himself, either. He'd come back from the rail camp early, bursting into the clearing, his face puffy and streaked with dirt and tears. He'd started to tell her about something that had happened at work, but she'd cut him off, telling him they could talk about it later, but right now she had an awful feeling Herc had done something bad.

Stef had muttered, 'Typical,' and disappeared into his hut, reaching to slam the door before remembering there wasn't one, and then stamping so hard it sent the crow flapping off in outrage.

She guessed Benadrylla had said no to changing the route. Well, no surprises there – it had always been a forlorn hope.

And now, things turned out to be even worse than they'd thought, because her investigative trip to Little

Wazzock had revealed that the tracks on that side had already been laid, almost as far as the clearing. They had simply not noticed before, having had no reason to venture out that way. The noise of people and machines echoed around, and they had assumed it was all coming from the Sad Sack side.

It wasn't clear what would happen when both sets of tracks reached the clearing. As long as the man from FUN was observing, Benadrylla would surely not dare hurt the children. But the law suddenly seemed a very fragile and insubstantial thing in comparison with the might of Crumplepatch Industries.

Ashna had come back from Sad Sack even more convinced that Bickley Brimstone was the one they should be worrying about. 'He's definitely doing something to people – messing with their minds. I've asked Arfur to do some snooping.'

'Ashna, we kind of have bigger problems here,' Tig told her. 'Bickley isn't about to invade Marshmallow. And you should stay away from his shop – it only makes you cough whenever you go in there.'

Nellie and Cuthbert's heist on Finnick's briefcase had yielded the work schedule which, alarmingly, claimed that the opening ceremony was to be held just a week from now. It had also yielded a FUN rubber stamp, which

Nellie had kept to give to Herc, as promised. It read APPROVED FUN in sensible, prudently spaced letters. No doubt he would be delighted with it, whenever he finally showed up.

As if summoned by his sister's thoughts, Herc burst through the trees. Then someone else staggered into view behind him – a boy in Crumplepatch uniform. The miserable one who had carried Benadrylla's basket of goodies. They all shot to their feet in alarm.

'Say hello to Joe!' Herc beamed around at them. 'He's come to live with us.'

The others began talking all at once.

'Where have you BEEN?' bellowed Tig over them all. 'And why have you brought *him*? He works for *her*.'

Herc flapped her questions away. 'Not anymore he doesn't. I went to get hay for Pamela, just like you said. That's all. I bumped into Joe on the way home, and rescued him.' He patted Pamela, who ignored everyone and bent her head to start on the hay. 'Well, actually, I bumped into the person who was chasing him with a whip.'

Tig narrowed her eyes and glanced at Joe, who said, 'It's true.' He shook his head in disbelief. 'He dropped out of the sky, right on top of the goon. Knocked him out cold.'

'Completely on purpose,' Herc clarified.

Cuthbert frowned. 'Why was he chasing you?'

Joe's expression darkened. 'The rail camp's been flattened by a herd of stampeding cows. And the boss blames me, because I was meant to be keeping an eye on things. It was your friend who sabotaged half her equipment.'

Ashna frowned sceptically. 'Stef sabotaged the equipment? *Stef* did it?' She exchanged a look of confusion with Tig.

'Anyway, he just ran off, so she took it out on me.'

Tig's face broke into a grin. 'I guess she refused to back down and Stef decided to get on with it after all. But that's brilliant! Her plans are ruined.'

'*I* did the cows bit, actually,' Herc put in proudly, now that this was a good thing. He loved it when it turned out he was even more of a genius than he'd thought. 'I saved Marshmallow.'

'Wouldn't go that far. She'll be back,' Joe told them. 'She won't just give up, you know. She'll . . . she'll . . .' He swayed, held out his hand to lean on Herc, but missed him and toppled over.

Tig rushed to his side. 'You're hurt,' she said, noting a cut on his head, bruises swelling.

Herc scampered to fetch some water.

When Joe had drained the glass, leaning back against

129

the wall of Tig's hut and closing his eyes in relief, Tig asked, 'Benadrylla told that bloke to hurt you?'

He nodded weakly. 'I've known for ages she wanted an excuse to get rid of me.'

Tig felt a surge of anger. 'Well, don't you worry. You're with us now. We'll protect you.'

She stepped away to fetch Stef, in the hope that he'd calmed down now. He must have just been scared, after all that had happened. Her heart squeezed a little. They seemed to have grown apart, lately. Well, they couldn't afford to do that anymore. They'd all have to work together on this.

Ashna followed her. 'At least we have a bit of breathing space, now. Sounds like she'll need time to make repairs.'

Unfortunately, that was all the breathing space they got, because at that moment Benadrylla Crumplepatch strode into the clearing, with the man from FUN scampering after her.

✎ Chapter Sixteen ✎

'W'ell, well, well,' Benadrylla said, her diamond earrings glinting as she flicked aside a blonde curl that had stuck to her temple. Her skin was flushed and a little shiny with perspiration, but she didn't seem overwrought or upset. If anything, it was as though energy were zipping through her, confidence and triumph in her every gesture. 'What do we have here, Finnick? Are these *buildings*?' She placed her palm just under her collarbone with a dramatic flourish. 'I was not expecting *those* here!'

Tig surreptitiously checked behind her – Joe had disappeared, and there was no sign of Stef either, thankfully.

'Wow, you have a really bad memory,' Herc piped up. 'You should write things down in a diary or something, so you don't forget them.'

'What do you want?' Ashna asked bluntly.

Benadrylla's gaze swept over the area. 'I've lost two of my workers. I have an idea they might have headed this way.'

Nellie examined her fingernails. 'Nope, haven't seen anyone. Anything else?'

'Well, yes, since you ask. Children, I'm afraid your time here is up.'

'You can't touch us,' Cuthbert said quietly. 'We're not going anywhere.'

'Yes to the first, and no to the second!' Benadrylla beamed. 'Because soon you will have no shelter. Finnick, in that little folder of yours, do you see any *planning permission* for buildings in this area?'

Finnick was already rooting through his papers, frowning. 'Ah, no. It has not been applied for.'

Tig's stomach dropped through her boots. Benadrylla had found a loophole of her own.

Benadrylla's smile widened. 'Oh! Whereas I *do* have planning permission.' She fished in her dress pocket, drew out a folded sheet of paper, and waved it at them. 'To build my railway right through this very spot. And I have permission to destroy any obstacle that lies in its path . . . Correct?' She paused for effect, and made sure everyone was listening.

Finnick cleared his throat. 'Provided all the appropriate protective headgear is worn and—'

'*Thank* you.'

Herc clutched at his sister in horror.

'No . . .' Tig breathed. 'Please. You can't.'

'Oh yes I—' A loud rip stopped Benadrylla mid-breath, and she looked down. A hole had appeared in her dress, where Pamela had taken a fancy to its flowery frills. A small but intense tug of war ensued, the result of which was that the goat sauntered back to Herc with almost the entire back half of the fabric, while Benadrylla screeched in fury and tried to hold the dress together.

Herc examined the material. 'Ah, blackberries. She loves those.'

Finnick wasn't sure why he felt so uncomfortable – Benadrylla was entirely right about the planning permission. It was certainly unfortunate that the boy who had shown such an interest in kerning turned out to be living here, but that couldn't be it; feeling bad for the children was less important than being correct. So he was relieved when, during the distraction caused by the goat, he realized that he could do something even *more* correct.

'Ahem,' he said. 'There is just one problem.'

Benadrylla's spotlight gaze swung his way, making Finnick turn bright red. She was clearly not in the mood

for more problems – not when everyone could see her knickers.

He drew out another sheet from his files – the map of Knott Wood. 'The thing is, Ms Crumplepatch, you obtained permission to cut down the *trees*. You didn't ask for a *buildings* demolition permit, because there is nothing to demolish.'

Benadrylla's eyebrows crumpled in irritation. 'I'm talking about these ridiculous huts, you fool. Just give me permission to destroy those, then.'

Finnick tried to moisten his lips with his dry tongue.

'Technically . . . I can't. There are no buildings on the map here, as you can see. So, as far as the Ministry is concerned, they don't exist.' He warily moved the map in front of her and pointed his trembling finger at the swathe of green that denoted the clearing. 'You cannot destroy non-existent obstacles. Article forty-two point six of the FUN code is quite clear.'

Benadrylla thrust out her gloved hand to point his chin, none too gently, in the direction of Marshmallow. 'It's before your very eyes!'

Finnick addressed her out of the only part of his mouth that could move under her iron grip. 'But it's . . . not . . . on . . . the . . . map.'

Benadrylla made a strangled sound and flailed with her free arm out in front of her while the other shook his head till his brain rattled. 'Just LOOK!'

But Finnick's eyes were rolling around, focusing everywhere except in front of him, as if Marshmallow were the head of Medusa and might turn him to stone. 'No, no . . . they've coloured it in light green. That means grass. If there were buildings, they'd be brown squares.'

Every now and then this happened, when you worked for FUN – a nightmarish void would open up between reality and the paperwork; less experienced FUN officers had fallen into it, never to be seen again. Not Finnick.

135

When it came to choosing between the real world and paperwork, for him there was no contest. The time had come to stand up for what was right. Or at least what was stamped and filed.

He held his folder in front of him like a shield. 'Physical facts cannot be allowed to complicate the situation. FUN has ruled that there are no buildings in the woods, and that's final. The map is very clear. Any attempt to destroy these non-existent buildings illegally will result in your entire operation being shut down. Now I must go and lie down. I have a headache.'

He released himself from her grip and walked with dignity out of the clearing, swaying slightly with the sheer purity of the bureaucracy he'd just delivered.

Benadrylla did not hang around long after Finnick's departure, restricting herself to a murderous glare and a promise that they hadn't heard the end of this.

When she'd gone, there was whooping and cheering until Stef interrupted with a furious shout. 'How do we know he's not a spy?'

They all turned in surprise to see him half dragging Joe out of the old toilet bush where he had dived to hide.

Nobody spoke. They seemed paralysed with shock – Stef knew his face was probably blotchy from crying, but he didn't care. Now he was all rage.

'He's just turned up, he's one of *them*, and you're going to welcome him in, no questions asked? Well, I'm not helping make a hut for him, I'll tell you that now. I'm not the soft touch you all seem to think I am.' He let go of Joe's shirt with a disgusted grunt, and Joe moved away from him warily.

The awkward silence continued; none of them appeared to know what to say. It was as though an entirely different person had stepped out of Stef's hut.

It was Tig who broke it. 'Thing is, Stef, I'd be with you on that normally, except . . . well, you must've heard Benadrylla just now. She's no friend of his, believe me.'

Joe squinted up at Stef. 'You're the reason I'm here in the first place. She blamed me for all that equipment you trashed.'

Stef couldn't believe what he was hearing. 'You set me up!'

'I just . . . You were annoying me. Swanning around all day, the big favourite. I *needed* that job and I could see she was shaping up to kick me out. So I wanted to show that you didn't know what you were doing. Which you don't. I mean – I didn't *do* anything, I just let *you* do it.'

'On purpose, so she would turn on me. You knew what sort of person she is.'

Joe laughed, and then winced, clutching his ribs. 'You've changed your tune! Guess you found yourself on her bad side, hey? Well, newsflash: she doesn't have a good side. It's all an act.'

'I know that now,' Stef snapped, but his voice cracked on the last word. His bottom lip was trembling. 'She made me think that I . . . Well, I believed her and . . .'

138

He faltered, blinking against the warmth in his eyes that threatened tears again, summoning back the anger instead. 'And I'm not going to make the same mistake with *you*. I'm thinking this is all a bit suspicious, you turning up here. Bit of a coincidence.'

He saw glances pass between the others. He could tell what they were all thinking: *He's paranoid.* Well, maybe. Better than being gullible. Better than being a soft touch. He was done with all that. No more trusting anyone, ever.

'Stef . . .' Ashna began. 'That doesn't make any sense.'

Herc tapped Stef on the arm. 'Joe's telling the truth. Benadrylla sent someone to hurt him.'

'It'll be a trap.' Stef's mouth set in a hard line, a muscle flickering in his cheek, making his scar ripple. 'A few bruises, to make him look convincing.'

'Hey, that's enough.' Tig was firm.

'I understand.' Joe winced. He sounded reasonable, conciliatory. 'I hurt his pride, so he's angry. And, to be fair, I mean, it *is* the kind of thing she'd do. Don't worry, I'll find somewhere else to go. I don't want to be any trouble. Thanks for hiding me just then.'

Tig was furious. 'You're staying right here. What's got into you, Stef? Honestly, one minute Benadrylla's an angel who can do no wrong, and when it turns out she isn't, you flip and won't even trust anyone who's been within a mile of her. Can't you just be sensible for once? Find some middle ground?'

Stef let out a sharp exhalation, almost a laugh. 'Well, all I can say is watch out, you lot. Keep an eye on your stuff, in case he steals it. And he can make his own stupid shelter.'

With a vicious kick at the earth that sent dust flying up around him, Stef stuck his hands in his pockets and strode off to the other side of the clearing.

He heard Herc's worried voice behind him. 'I think Benadrylla must have hit Stef on the head.' He sounded tearful. 'He's gone wrong.'

❧ Chapter Seventeen ❧

Over the following few days, nobody in Marshmallow was celebrating their temporary escape.

The atmosphere was unsettling, crackling with discontent, like electricity building in the air before a storm. Stef was tucked away in his hut whittling away randomly at sticks with his knife, only emerging grudgingly to cook food when it was his turn. The others treated him warily, as though *he* was the stranger in their midst. Joe, by contrast, was amiable, helpful, and refused to return Stef's rudeness, ignoring his glares. He spent an hour that first day making a rudimentary shelter with Tig's help, and declared himself perfectly satisfied with it, despite the fact that it was really just twigs and a tarpaulin, and he'd woken up dew-damp from head to toe each morning. It was at the very furthest edge of the clearing, as far away as possible from the other huts. 'Don't want to tread on anyone's toes,' Joe had said ruefully, and they all knew who he meant.

All around them the shouts of lumberjacks and the thwack of axes on trunks grew ever closer, as Crumplepatch Railways worked at triple speed making repairs to the ruined camp, continuing their relentless progress. The stench and haze of coal-smoke was everywhere, like a low mist, causing Ashna's chronic cough to worsen. A wide path was growing, stretching out from the camp towards them, and along it crept a shine of metal tracks. It was only a matter of time before they reached Marshmallow.

And then what? For the moment there was stalemate, the children protected by the invisible walls of the clearing and Finnick's bizarre ruling, but surely Joe was right: Benadrylla would keep looking for a way to burst that fragile bubble.

Herc was driving Tig mad, having grown bored of the FUN stamp. He'd been so excited to use it at first, stamping everything from tree trunks to the Marshmallow sign. Even his own elbows claimed to be APPROVED FUN. Now it lay discarded, and he was following her around, whining about being bored.

Tig was on the verge of snapping his head off, when Joe offered to take him over to the other side of the clearing to play.

Tig grunted non-committally. She appreciated the

thought, but he wouldn't get anywhere. Stef was the only person who might have a chance of keeping Herc's attention, but *he* was still sulking.

Why was nobody except her focusing on the task at hand: saving them all from Benadrylla?

Tig had suggested they all have a strategy meeting that evening. When a sudden rain shower drenched the site, she, Ashna, Cuthbert, Nellie and a reluctant Stef squeezed inside the second-largest hut, since the largest was full of Herc's marshmallow-making gear.

Tig began. 'The railway opening will be delayed, I suppose, but we need to think about how to stop it completely.'

'Where's Joe?' asked Ashna, panting a little. The rain had dampened down some of the smoke that irritated her lungs so much, but the air was far from fresh. 'He's been around Benadrylla for a while – he might be able to give us some idea of what she might do next.'

Stef snapped back. 'Yeah. Because he's almost certainly in on it. Have you noticed he keeps going for walks? I bet he's reporting back.'

Nellie rolled her eyes. 'Give it a rest. We all know you're not exactly a fan. No wonder he feels the need to get away.'

At that moment Joe arrived with Herc, who was happily chatting away to him, rolling a marshmallow between his fingers, nipping it between his teeth and seeing how far it would stretch. They squashed in against the others, and the pressure against the walls made them creak ominously.

'I've been telling Joe how I make the marshmallows,' Herc told them. 'He says he's never tasted anything as good.' He smiled shyly for confirmation at Joe, who fist-bumped him.

Tig could practically feel Stef bristling next to her.

'Herc,' she said, judging that planning anything would be a lot simpler without her brother's interventions, 'we're just going to be having a discussion about the railway business in here. You can join in, if you like. There's going to be a lot of talk about finances, examining Benadrylla's accounts, and adding up numbers in columns.' She held out a pencil.

Herc didn't need telling twice. He disappeared.

Tig sighed with relief. 'Thanks, Joe, for keeping him out of trouble today for me. Gave me some time to think.'

Stef made a short *pff* sound and rolled his eyes. 'Joe didn't *do* anything. Herc just likes talking about marshmallows. Anyone could've distracted him by doing that.'

'Yeah? So why didn't you, then?' Joe asked Stef, his head tilted to one side.

Stef flinched as though he'd been punched.

Cuthbert licked his lips. 'O*kaaay*, let's keep this nice and polite. I'll write down what everyone says – that always makes people think before they speak.'

'Ooh, like in a courtroom,' Nellie said.

Joe sighed wearily, as though he were the sole adult in a room full of toddlers. 'Let's get this over with. What do you want to know?'

'I suppose, what Benadrylla might do next,' said Tig. 'Is there any chance we could come to an agreement with her? Wouldn't that be easier for her?'

Joe shook his head. 'No chance at all.' He glanced around at them. 'Dunno why you think I'm the expert – she never exactly shared her innermost thoughts with me. But if you want my opinion, you're over-thinking this. She just doesn't like it when people get in her way. She takes it personally.'

Stef sniffed. 'Like *you* do when someone gets in *your* way?'

'Not this again . . .'

Ashna cleared her throat. 'Let's put that to one side for a second. I'm convinced Bickley Brimstone is involved with the railway somehow. He's always hanging around Benadrylla, and he's hypnotizing everyone in Sad Sack.'

Nellie rolled her eyes. 'There you go again. Just

145

because Ma Yeasty got the 'ump wiv you, you think he must've hypnotized her. I doubt it, but so what if he has? It's probably the only way he can make everyone think he's a great bloke and sell more of his stupid potions. It just makes him even more of a pathetic fake. It's harmless.'

'It's not only that. Bickley's really interested in the railway. It's all connected, somehow.'

Nellie guffawed. 'Yeah. Maybe Ma Yeasty's working as a secret agent. Maybe Crumplepatch Railways is using her broccoli muffins to poison Benadrylla's enemies—'

'Never mind Ma Yeasty,' broke in Cuthbert. 'I'm worried about Finnick. He fought off Benadrylla admirably, even if it was only to keep the paperwork in order, but from what Joe says, she'll try to find a way round him. We should figure out how.'

Stef screwed up his face in irritation. 'Why are you all going on about Finnick and Ma Yeasty? Are you not listening to me? Joe's a spy, I'm telling you.'

Tig grimaced, exasperated. 'Will you *please* give it a rest, Stef. We're all on the same side here.' She laid a restraining hand on his arm.

'That's my point. We're not.'

'I've had enough of this,' Joe said. 'I said I was sorry for letting Stef get in trouble. I explained why. I can't do any more.' He struggled to his feet to leave. Unfortunately, there were several sets of legs in Joe's path, and Stef's elbow caught him squarely on the chin as he shook off Tig's hand. Joe whirled round and shoved him back, pushing him into Nellie, who yelled 'Oi!' and kicked out, catching Cuthbert's shin. Cuthbert yanked his leg back and overbalanced into Ashna, who shouted 'Stop!' but instantly found herself at the bottom of a scuffling, sprawling heap full of sharp nails and hard heads colliding with increasing howls of pain and outrage. It only dispersed when Herc threw a bucket of water on them.

'Can you keep it down?' he complained, as they gasped into silence, dripping. 'I need to concentrate. I'm making chamomile marshmallows for Pamela.'

The atmosphere in camp as they ate was awkward.

Joe and Stef sat on opposite sides of the fire, pointedly ignoring each other. It was only at bedtime, when they were peeling away to their own shelters, that Joe passed near to Stef and paused.

'You're wrong about me, you know. Apart from one thing: I don't like you. You're right about that.'

Stef merely scowled into the dying embers of the fire, not giving him the satisfaction of a response.

Joe leaned down so that his head was just above Stef's. 'But the thing is, everyone else is happy I'm here. Herc likes me, and I'm helping him.'

It was undeniable. And if Stef were honest, that was what hurt most of all.

Joe stood up straight again and muttered over his shoulder, 'So if anyone should leave, it's you.'

⚈ *Chapter Eighteen* ⚈

Finnick held his brand new APPROVED FUN stamp above the map.

The stamp had freshly arrived from the Ministry, with a stern note from Stapleford Pinch, the Head Minister for FUN himself, reprimanding him for losing the other one. His punishment was to miss the feast that would be held before the railway opening ceremony. Oh, the shame of it! He was lucky, really, he knew: careers had been ended for less. He still couldn't figure out how it had happened, any of it – the disappearance of his briefcase, and then its return minus the precious stamp.

His hand was trembling slightly, now.

It wasn't just that Benadrylla was standing so close to him, those pale, slender fingers drumming on the table. It wasn't even that she'd brought along two of the bigger lumberjacks with her, and they had brought their axes indoors with them, without a sponge cover. It was the map; something about it made him feel sick.

A lot of people thought that the bureaucrats of FUN didn't have feelings. They assumed that being such sticklers for correctness, and doing things by the book, the officials must have laid aside their emotions long ago.

Those people were extremely mistaken.

Far from blunting his senses, Finnick's years at FUN had honed them to a very fine point. A tick in the wrong place on a form gave him an actual headache; an answer scribbled over the edges of a box filled him with a sense of impending doom; a paper misfiled sent his heart racing and his blood pressure soaring.

This map had brought him out in a clammy sweat. It hurt his eyeballs and dried his tongue. There was something so very wrong about it, but he couldn't tell what it was. Through the ringing in his ears he heard Benadrylla's voice.

'So as you can see, this is the *correct* map, showing the buildings in Knott Wood that you were for some reason unable to see. It seems your other one was . . . mis-drawn. Those dwellings are part of an old, abandoned settlement. It's official.'

Finnick wiped the sweat from his eyes and tried to focus. There they were: brown squares for buildings, and above them, in beautifully neat script: *Abandoned Village.* The initials H.H.H. declared that the mapmaker was none other than Hildegaard Hillfinger of Hubbashire – famous for her meticulous cartography, the most beautifully accurate mapping in the country. She was something of a hero at FUN. They had a large framed picture of her at HQ, in

which she was holding her famous diamond-encrusted gold compass and calipers, engraved *H.H.H.* They'd had to put glass over the portrait to protect it from drool stains. He'd recognize her maps anywhere, and this was one. 'I don't understand. The other map . . .'

'Was incorrect. Don't worry. I won't tell anyone you've been using the wrong one.' She winked.

He felt bile rise in his throat. 'I should . . . check. Let me just post a message to Professor Hillfinger to confirm. I'll mark it urgent – it'll be there in a day or two.'

'She's on holiday,' said one of the lumberjacks, leaning his axe against the table in order to crack his knuckles. 'Went away just after we paid her a visit.'

Benadrylla leaned over him so that her perfume invaded his nostrils and made it hard to breathe. 'Stamp the map. And then the form to destroy the buildings.'

He was breathing heavily now, his vision swimming in and out. If he stamped it with his FUN stamp, the children's village in the woods would be official, so

Benadrylla could officially crush it to smithereens. But Hildegaard's mapping could not be denied. There was no higher authority.

Finnick was hazy about what happened next, because he passed out shortly afterwards. When he awoke, the FUN stamp was still clutched in his stiff, ink-stained fingers, but the map and the permission form were gone, along with his visitors.

Only a faint scent of lavender remained.

❧ Chapter Nineteen ❧

Bickley Brimstone was about to shut up shop for the night. It was nearly midnight – he'd had so many customers lately that he'd had to extend his opening hours. He was about to empty the till, stuffed full of the day's takings, when a final customer turned up and slapped a coin on the counter.

Bickley lifted his chin in order to better be able to look down his nose. 'Oh, it's *you*!' He made a show of shutting the till and locking it.

'True,' Arfur said. 'But, not being funny, I was hoping to be told somefink I don't already know. That it, then? Cos if it is, I'll have me money back.'

Brimstone's hand came out and covered the coin faster than a striking snake. 'Of course that's not *it*. I did not expect to see you in here. Of all people.'

They eyed each other warily. Brimstone knew that Arfur had misled him about the St Halibut's children, and

Arfur knew that Brimstone knew. Not only that, Brimstone knew that Arfur knew he knew. The knowledge hovered in the air between them like a thunderous fart in a library: unspeakable, potent, and accusing.

'How are your pigeons?' Bickley asked, with a smirk.

Arfur grew still.

This afternoon he'd come home from visiting his friend Lotta Gangrene, who managed the rubbish dump some miles outside Sad Sack, and went to top up the pigeons' feed. He'd found the coop empty. Not a single pigeon. This was a little unusual, but he'd thought perhaps they'd all just gone out to stretch their wings. But they were nowhere nearby. Not in the alley, not even on the awning of Powders 'n' Potions. The skies of Sad Sack were empty. His heart had quickened, but he'd kept telling himself they were birds, they were free, they could do what they liked. But something felt off, and pidge-napping was just the sort of thing Bickley might try, in revenge for the poop defacing his shop sign.

'They're great,' Arfur said, forcing a cheery tone. 'I'll tell 'em you was asking after 'em.'

The pharmacist chuckled. 'So. You are finally here to have your fortune told. Or perhaps there is something wrong with you? Other than the incurable sleaziness.'

'I'm curious, innit?' Arfur shrugged, letting his gaze

drift over the shelves of useless remedies. There was no sign of anything unusual. No stray feathers, or faint sounds of cooing from a cupboard. There were just the usual jars of dried leaves, packets of pills, and vials of potions. He plucked a small glass bottle at random and held it towards the light. The clear liquid sloshed inside. 'People what should know better are yappin' on and on about these skills of yours.'

Bickley's nose lifted a fraction further. 'So you do not believe I truly know the future? That my tea has miraculous properties? You do not have an open mind?'

Arfur twisted the bottle in his fingers to read the label: *Water of Healing: cures diarrhoea, rashes, stomach ache, depression, fever, hair loss, fungus. Also cleans pots and pans.* He reckoned only the 'water' bit was accurate. 'I don't like to leave nothin' open round here – there's a lot of crooks about.'

The pharmacist bristled and snatched the bottle from him, replacing it on the shelf. 'Well, you would know. I don't *have* to serve you, you know. I can refuse your money.'

'True!' said Arfur cheerfully. 'Give it back, then.' He held out his palm and twitched his fingers in invitation for the coin.

Bickley's fist tightened over the money. 'Oh, all right. I'll do it, but only because you begged me.' The pharmacist carefully locked the front door, and glanced down the street both ways before pulling the blind down. 'So. What ails you, Arfur?'

'Eh? Oh, let's say . . . I'm stressed out by working on the mobile library.' Arfur rubbed his hands and leaned on the counter. This was going to be fun. It was easily worth a quid to be able to poke fun at a swindler and expose him, as long as the swindler wasn't himself. And if Bickley

had taken the pigeons, they'd be here somewhere.

'Come with me.'

Bickley beckoned him round the counter, where he held open the door to the back room. A draught brushed past Arfur's neck as he walked into the dingy office and he shivered.

Bickley lit a couple of sticks of incense in a jar on the floor. A cinnamon smell wafted from them.

'Like setting fire to things, don't ya?' Arfur meant to speak chirpily, but his own voice sounded to him like a lonely echo in a cave. 'What you want that stink for? You just done a whoopsie in here or somethin'?'

Bickley smiled tightly. 'The smell will relax you.' He took up a china teapot from the table in front of them. 'Make yourself comfortable.' Then he left through the door that led upstairs to his living quarters.

On the table in front of Arfur stood a tiny cup and a wicker mat where the teapot had been. Two chairs were placed ready and waiting either side of the table, one pulled slightly out.

No pigeons. Maybe he should find a way to slip upstairs to check out the flat? He wasn't sure how, though. He might have to come back and break in tomorrow while Bickley was out front in the shop.

Arfur licked his lips. An oil lamp flickered on the

mantelpiece, casting rippling shadows. A clock quietly noted each second on the wall by the window, where a curtain was pulled all the way across, cutting off the world outside. He didn't like the subdued ticking noise it made, like someone *tut-tutting* in disapproval, the brass pendulum swinging from side to side tauntingly. He found he was moving his own head in time with it, and stopped, dropping abruptly into the chair. He nearly jumped out of it when the clock chimed, a tinkly little tune he'd heard somewhere before.

Somehow, of a sudden, he didn't fancy sitting down. In fact, he didn't fancy doing any of it. The hairs were prickling on his neck.

But he was here for the kids, he reminded himself – the cheeky little berks. Or for Ashna, at least. And if he could set her mind at rest, she'd stop giving him earache every time they met. Besides, since they'd talked, it *had* niggled at him, a little, if he were honest. Best just check Bickley wasn't up to anything weird. Or weirder than usual, anyway.

Ugh, it did stink in here, though. Tiny curls of smoke twisted lazily from the ends of the incense, the air above wobbling and hazy.

His eyelids felt heavy. He had a strong urge to fling open the window and breathe deeply. Come to that, fling

159

open the door and head home, quick smart. Never mind the kids; they were always telling him they could shift for themselves, weren't they?

The clock chimed again, repeating its annoying little tune. How long had he been here? He wasn't sure. Time had gone all slippery. But the clock must go off every few minutes or something. Crikey. That would drive him up the wall.

He was about to stand when he became aware that Brimstone was already sitting in the other chair. His stomach lurched. When had he come back in?

A delicate shimmer of steam rose from the spout of the teapot on the table; the china lid clinked as the contents were poured. The clock ticked, ticked, ticked. The incense was in his nostrils, creeping into his sinuses. Arfur had felt shivery but now he was hot, his tongue stuck to the roof of his mouth. He loosened his collar with a trembling finger. 'Phew!' he tried to say jovially, but it came out as a croak. 'I've got a thirst on!'

The pharmacist nodded in understanding as he pushed the cup across to him, and Arfur looked down into the translucent yellow liquid. Brown flaky petals swirled slowly at the bottom. Warmth rose, moisture clinging to his face.

'What sorta tea is it?'

'Just chamomile. For relaxation.'

Arfur licked his lips.

Bickley sighed. 'You're thirsty. So drink, while I talk. Let's see if we can ease your mind about those library books.'

It was pitch black when Stef awoke, heart battering against his chest. A nightmare, the claws of it still sharp and plucking at his nerves. In the dream, he'd brought an injured deer home and laid it gently on blankets in the midst of Marshmallow . . . but when he looked at the faces of his friends, he saw only horror. And when he turned back to the deer, he realized it wasn't a deer, but a huge, hungry wolf. They all ran for their lives, followed by the sounds of its pursuit, gaining on them through the trees. One by one, his friends cried out behind him, caught, but he kept running until he was the only one left. It was all his fault. All his . . .

He sat up and drew his palm across the back of his neck, drenched with sweat.

For a moment he thought it was the dream that had woken him, but then he heard Tig's voice from outside the hut, shouting for him.

'Get up. Something's happened.'

The others were emerging sleepily from their huts as the two of them approached Joe's lone makeshift shelter at the edge of the clearing. Even from a distance the damage was obvious – the branches lay smashed and scattered on the ground, the rubber sheet hurled to one side. There was a trail of squashed grass and churned mud leading from it, as though someone had been dragged out.

'I heard something, but I thought it was just an animal at first,' Tig told him, her voice tight.

Stef shivered, thinking of his dream.

'But then I heard a scream. I came out, but I was too late, too far away. They've taken him, Stef. Benadrylla's got Joe.'

At that moment a terrible wail of pain and despair cut through the darkness close by.

Herc!

Tig and Stef were at his side in half a second, dreading what they might find. Herc was standing where the path met the clearing, his face streaked with tears, pointing at something at his feet.

One forked branch had been left stuck into the muddy ground, and looped deliberately over the top of it was a familiar pink collar.

Chapter Twenty

Ashna watched Stef warily out of the corner of her eye as they walked down Sad Sack High Street together.

'Slow down, will you?' she panted. 'I can't . . .' Today her breathing was worse, her lungs protesting at the constant assault of smoke from the railway work. If she didn't take care, she might pass out. Already pinpricks of light were flashing at the corners of her vision, and her chest had to work to pull in air. She hated mentioning it – the last thing she wanted was to give her friends any more reason to worry. But Stef knew her well enough. He reduced his pace.

'It's my fault,' he muttered, angrily wiping his sleeve across his eyes. Any feeling of relief that Joe was gone had quickly ebbed away when he saw evidence of the violence that had taken place.

And of course there was Pamela's pink collar, left there

to mock them. Not trampled into the mud, not caught on a bush, where Pamela might just have shrugged it off on her own, but clean, buckled, neatly placed where they would not miss it. At first, Herc had refused to believe it, running, panting, out into the woods calling her name while Tig chased after him. It was almost worse when he finally gave up, understanding that Benadrylla had Pamela as well as Joe in her clutches. When Stef and Ashna had left that morning, the sounds of Herc's sobbing had followed them through the trees until they were too far to hear. He wouldn't eat, not even a marshmallow.

Having failed to move them out using flattery, persuasion, and then the law, Benadrylla was taking direct action to intimidate them into submitting to her will. Now that she had given up all pretence, Stef understood that there was real danger behind her threats. All his antipathy towards Joe felt suddenly petty, just a case of his own hurt pride. Of *course* Joe was insecure, defensive, deceiving . . . he had been desperate not to get into trouble with his boss – he knew what she was really like. Shamed at having been fooled by Benadrylla, Stef had taken out his anger on a fellow victim.

He felt sick and he had been crying for most of their journey, tears falling freely. 'We've got to get them back.'

Ashna squeezed his hand. 'We will. Arfur will help.'

Arfur liked to joke around, but when things got bad there was no one more seriously cunning.

When they arrived at his library cart, Arfur seemed to be sorting the stock – the books lay in piles on the ground while Bernard the pony stood hitched to the cart with an expression of immense boredom.

'Arfur, you've got to help us! Benadrylla Crumplepatch kidnapped our friend Joe last night. Or at least her goons did. And she's got Pamela, too.'

The con man looked up briefly over a pile of books he was holding and frowned in consternation. 'Budge over, would ya?' He hesitated for a moment between two boxes, then dumped the books in one and reached for more from the pile. 'Joe? I know they caught some kid stealing from the camp last night. Would that be him?'

Ashna stared at him. 'What did you hear?'

'Overheard a couple of off-duty Crumplepatch lumberjacks talking, early this morning on the high street. He weren't kidnapped, though – these blokes caught him fair and square, by all accounts, red-handed. Threw him in the back of a carriage and took him away. Shoulda known he'd be a friend of you lot.' He winked.

'That must be him! But he wasn't stealing anything. He was staying with us.'

Arfur frowned. 'Well, I dunno about that. They said

he's some spoilt rich kid they'd had trouble with before. Teenagers with money – they're always the worst for nicking stuff, I find.' Arfur said this with an entirely straight face, presumably disapproving less of thievery than of a teenager having money in the first place.

Stef grabbed his arm urgently. 'This boy – do you know where he is now?'

Arfur picked out two of the last books still in the cart and seemed reluctant to put them down. Then he shoved them in a box, too. 'They drove him straight back to his mum, apparently – she's staying at the Palatial, would you believe. I expect she's relieved to have him back, the scallywag.'

'Back with his . . . That's not his mother! It's Benadrylla! They must have said that so no one would question why they were taking him to her.'

But Arfur didn't appear to be listening. 'Posh plonker.' He tutted, then peered at Ashna, who was wheezing. 'You all right? You look a bit peaky. I'd offer you a rest in the cart but I got to get these books packed and out to the dump.'

Ashna had been about to set Arfur straight about Joe, but his words brought her up short. 'You . . . you're taking them to the dump?' Sad Sack's dump was in the desolate wasteland to the south, a few miles away – a lonely place piled high with the unwanted bits and pieces of Sad Sackers' lives. The stinking pile of rubbish was presided over by Lotta Gangrene, whose sense of smell had luckily disappeared years ago.

Ashna was not the only one to notice something amiss. Stef was looking at the coop, frowning. 'Where are your pigeons, Arfur?'

'Oh, off somewhere. They'll be back.' Ashna thought she heard the tiniest crack in his voice, but he showed no other sign of concern.

She felt dizzy. A horrible thought struck her. He was not the first person to have started behaving oddly lately. Taking his beloved books to the dump definitely counted as odd.

'You went to see Bickley Brimstone, didn't you? After I asked you to.' Her chest felt as though it were being squeezed in a giant fist.

'Sure did. And you can stop worrying about him, you know. I went and did his tea malarkey and you was completely wrong. It's just a load of jiggery-pokery, exactly like what I said.'

'Are you sure? What did he do? What did he say?'

Arfur paused for a moment and squinted upwards, thinking. Then he shook his head. 'Blowed if I can remember, it were that boring. Just rattled on and on

167

and on like a ruddy train, as he does. If he *were* trying to hypnotize me, it didn't have no effect. None whatsoever. Think I might even have nodded off. So there ya go – completely harmless.' He began whistling – a familiar six-note tune that made Ashna's blood freeze. The chime of the pharmacist's clock.

She and Stef stared at each other in horror. They both knew, without a doubt, that Arfur could not help them anymore. Whatever Bickley Brimstone had done to him, he could no longer be trusted.

Ashna's head pounded; her vision darkened. The last thing she saw before she passed out were Stef's and Arfur's concerned faces looming above.

enadrylla watched Stapleford Pinch, Head Minister for FUN, over her cup as she sipped her morning coffee in the lounge of the Palatial Hotel.

Pinch's conversation was so dull it was difficult to concentrate. He had shared his enthusiasm for the hotel's filing system (he had been handed the hotel's cleaning rota for the past six months and was planning to make it his bedtime read) and was now explaining cheerfully the benefits of using the correct size of staples for different administrative tasks. She'd thought Finnick was bad, but Pinch was on a whole new level. She wanted to take his briefcase and ram it into his head just so she wouldn't have to listen to his voice.

Nevertheless, he was Head Minister for FUN, and therefore, for now, had to be kept happy, along with all the other FUN officials staying at the Palatial. The tracks would be finished in the next few hours and tomorrow she could host the ceremony. Pinch would sign everything off, and she'd finally be paid. Then she'd never have to set foot in this stinking cesspit of a county again. At least she'd have gained a few more young workers for her coal mine up in Rankshire, which was running dangerously low on staff after some nasty accidents – those orphans wouldn't last long, but she'd get a few weeks out of them. Probably.

Her plan seemed to be working well. Earlier that morning the two lumberjacks had reported that Joe had been taken upstairs, where he could do no harm. The young fool had been angry, rude, and had put up a fight at first, but now he was subdued and resigned. He wouldn't cause any further trouble. He'd never been much good to her as a worker – constantly whining and getting things wrong – but now he would finally be of use.

As bait.

There was the orphans' goat, too, which for some unfathomable reason the lumberjacks had brought to her as well. She'd meant them to just steal it out of spite and then get rid of the creature, but the oafs had brought it here – to the hotel, of all places. She'd had the wretched thing taken to the kitchens; the chef could probably make something out of it. Leaving the collar behind after taking Joe had been a nice touch, though – just to drive home the

170

point, in case the children didn't get it. They weren't very bright, after all.

The pharmacist had suggested the plan, telling her the children's history, that they stuck together like limpets and would never abandon each other. She just hoped they'd become fond enough of Joe over the last few days to care what happened to him, and to attempt a rescue.

The children themselves were now the only obstacle in the completion of the railway. The obnoxious little berks would no doubt lie down in front of their precious huts, and that infuriating pen-pusher Finnick would object if she just ran the machines over them. Pinch had banned him from the feast for some trivial misdemeanour but, knowing Finnick, he would probably have stayed behind in the clearing anyway, to check she was keeping to the rules. If she didn't know better, she might think he was worried about the orphans.

The staff at the Palatial, as well as her own people, would be on the lookout for any children arriving, and then they could be contained. Her trap was set perfectly. The destruction of the huts would begin as soon as they all left the woods to come and save Joe.

Bickley Brimstone had been bitterly disappointed that she would not allow him to attend the feast at the Palatial today. He had turned up yesterday with a cageful of pigeons and had given them to the increasingly harassed chef with the suggestion he make pigeon soup with them. The chef had not been impressed. 'What is this, a zoo?' he complained, bewildered. 'I don't want to see anything that hasn't been through the butcher first.' Nevertheless, he had been persuaded to take them to the kitchen, grumpily.

The tiresome pharmacist had wanted to serve tea at the feast and give a speech to all the FUN officials; there was no question of her allowing this – they couldn't sign off the railway if they'd all been bored to death the day before. He had pestered and begged her, and she had only been able to get rid of him by promising to let him give an introduction at the opening ceremony tomorrow instead. And afterwards . . . well. Their aims had coincided temporarily, but Brimstone was a liability. He knew far too much – forcing Professor Hillfinger to make a new map had been his idea, but Benadrylla suspected he'd try to use it to blackmail her somehow. He'd have to be thrown overboard – possibly literally, once the trains were running. Accidents did happen, even on FUN-approved projects.

'Ms Crumplepatch?'

She realized Pinch was speaking to her. 'I'm sorry, Minister, I drifted off there. What were you saying?'

'I was just saying how much I had been looking forward

to the opening ceremony of the railway tomorrow. Only, I understand there has been some disruption – damage to the equipment, problems with permissions and so on. Will it be delayed?'

'No, Minister. I've just sorted that out. We're perfectly on schedule.' She smiled sweetly at him. 'I have people adding the finishing touches as we speak.'

⚈ Chapter Twenty-Two ⚈

The orphans knew they were getting close when the ride became smoother, all at once, as though Bernard had pulled the cart right off a cliff and was trotting on air.

The road from Sad Sack was pitted, full of loose stones, gaping holes, and at various points sloped at such an angle that if you didn't go slowly you'd tip right over – even if you were walking. It was a road that had let itself go years ago, as if it couldn't see the point of trying when all that lay at the end of it was a forgotten, stinking town in a forlorn part of the world.

Lardidar Valley, on the other hand, had airs and graces. It could not be more different from its unwashed and embarrassing neighbour. It was ten miles away, but if it could, it would have picked up its skirts and flounced another hundred.

The beginning of the smooth granite road was the first

indication that you were on the up. The next was a fancy stone arch held between two enormous stone lions on either side of the road, which you had to pass under to enter the town. On the arch a sign read: *Lardidar Valley: Please Wipe Your Feet.* Further in were the huge houses with marble columns, ornate iron gates and manicured lawns, with large dogs patrolling them. But before those, just after the archway, was the Palatial Hotel.

The Palatial was where you stayed if you had plenty of money and you were forced by circumstances beyond your control to visit Garbashire. If you wanted somewhere clean, with a bed you didn't have to share with six-legged biting creatures, there was literally nowhere else in the county to stay. The Palatial took itself very seriously, with liveried, bowing staff who never quite looked you in the eye in order to make you feel important. The carpets were thick, the room doors all closed with a throaty *clunk*, people spoke in low voices, as if the building itself demanded respect. It cost so much to take a room for the night that when they handed you your bill they put a chair behind you in case you needed to sit down. The main building was made of six storeys of white stone, the uppermost suites having balconies with ivy wound over their iron railings.

Stef slowed the cart so they could eyeball the hotel

entrance as they passed. It was swarming with FUN officials.

'That's odd,' said Tig. 'The feast must be going ahead after all. I thought they'd have to delay it because Benadrylla hasn't got permission to destroy Marshmallow.'

Cuthbert shifted uncomfortably. 'Perhaps it was too late to cancel the catering.'

'I wish Ashna was here,' fretted Nellie. 'She'd be shinning up them drainpipes and in through a window before you could say "break-in".'

Tig couldn't disagree. But Ashna was in no state to do such a thing. Stef and Arfur had taken her straight to the Mending House, and Maisie had put her into her own bed to ensure she had peace and quiet. Ashna had barely protested – that was how they knew her lungs must be *really* bad. But she'd insisted she'd be fine after a rest, away from the smoke and dust in the woods, and they knew better than to argue.

Before she'd sunk into sleep, she and Stef had had a whispered, urgent conversation. And then, while Maisie gave Arfur a severe telling-off for letting one of his children get into such a state, Stef had slipped out of the Mending House. He had taken the empty cart up to the edge of Knott Wood and left it out of sight near the path, before running all the way to Marshmallow with the news. It wasn't stealing, he reasoned, because he'd be giving the cart back. When they'd finished with it.

Initially, Tig and Stef had planned for just the two of them to go to the Palatial, to keep the mission discreet. But then Nellie had insisted it was at least a three-person job, Cuthbert pointed out that he and Nellie went everywhere together, and Herc had said Pamela was *his* goat, and if they tried to stop him coming, he'd bite them. It seemed safer to let them all come. Their home was protected for now, anyway, so they didn't need to stay to guard it.

Behind the Palatial were the stables where the horses of the wealthy could bed down in comfort, guarded by their own stable-hands, who stood rigid outside each pen, taking shifts day and night.

'That's where Pamela will be,' whispered Herc, his face pinched in fury, peering out the back of the cart as it trundled slowly past. 'The stables.'

'Shh,' Tig told him. 'We don't know that.' She didn't say that Pamela might not even be at the Palatial at all . . . Who knew what Benadrylla might have done with her?

Bernard pulled up a little distance from the hotel, where a copse of plum trees sheltered them from view, and they sat for a few minutes, watching through the branches as people came and went. There was a huge amount of activity, with carriages drawing up, luggage and people being unloaded. A small group of well-dressed men and women with FUN briefcases marched up to the main entrance and were ushered inside.

'This is bad,' Stef breathed, sweating. 'The whole Ministry of Fun is here. How are we going to get past them all and then out again with Joe?'

Cuthbert sat up straight suddenly. 'We don't. We only need to get *in* without being noticed, not out.'

They all stared at him, uncomprehending.

'We're going to stop the railway. Right here and now. Think about it. Benadrylla *kidnapped* Joe. FUN loves rules and she's just broken about a hundred of them by taking him. Once we've found him, he's our proof that she's broken the law in a big way. *Public* proof. No one will be able to brush it under the carpet.'

There was a long pause.

'You're right . . .' Tig said slowly. 'We can just show them Joe. Take him right to Stapleford Pinch and tell him all about what she did.' She grinned. 'Oh, she's going to be in *so* much trouble.'

Cuthbert grinned back. 'Let me handle that part. I speak the language of FUN.'

Nellie rubbed her hands. 'All *right*. But we do have to find him first. So we gotta figure out a way in.' She yanked a ripe plum from the tree and took a huge bite from it, juice dripping down her chin.

They sat and observed for a while, obscured by the trees.

On the nearest side of the hotel a large trolley heaped with laundry was stuck halfway through a door, and two men in the red and gold uniform of the Palatial shoved it forward and back clumsily. Bundles toppled off at their increasingly violent attempts, before the trolley suddenly shot inside, causing both men to fall over, cursing. The last one cast a cursory glance around before closing the door, pulling out a large bunch of keys on a chain.

'Staff entrance,' observed Tig. 'That's the only other outer door apart from the main entrance, and he's just locked it. We're not getting in that way. They're pretty hot on security.'

Tig parted the tree branches and looked through at the imposing facade of the Palatial. No fewer than four footmen were standing at the grand entrance, and there were undoubtedly more inside. She bet it was one of those places where you couldn't take a single step without someone asking if they could help you.

Joe was in there somewhere.

Her fists clenched.

Hold on. We're coming for you.

★

'When are they coming back?' Herc asked, again, twitching the curtain aside to ask the back of Stef's head in the driving seat.

Stef closed his eyes. 'I still don't know, Herc. Nothing's changed in the past minute. When they're done, OK?'

Tig and Nellie had gone to sneak into the building and find Joe, while Cuthbert was hiding behind pillars, focusing on listening to the conversations of the FUN officials, to learn the plan for the feast and exactly where Stapleford Pinch would be, so they could make maximum impact with their big reveal.

Stef understood why he'd been left with Herc. Someone needed to keep an eye on him or he'd surely go off by himself and get into trouble, ruining everything. Herc would undoubtedly be helpful in keeping Pamela under control once they had her; the last thing they needed was a goat on the loose.

Herc pulled back the curtain further to narrow his eyes at Stef. 'You've remembered to bring enough chamomile, right? Because she'll be stressed out and it'll help her feel better.'

Stef sighed, gesturing at his bulging pockets. 'I could *not* fit any more of it in there. I look like I'm wearing saddlebags.'

'And they're not just going to come back with Joe and

go, "Oh, we couldn't find Pamela, what a shame," are they? Because I'm not leaving without her.'

'Course not,' Stef reassured him. 'She's part of our family, isn't she?' This seemed to satisfy Herc, though if Pamela was a member of the family, then she was the grumpy great-aunt they all tried to avoid. Herc nodded and let the curtain drop again.

'Can we go and check, really quickly? Pamela is probably just round the—'

'Still no.'

'But—'

'No! Tig would kill me if I let you out of my sight.'

'So come with me.'

Through gritted teeth: 'One more time: we listen for the whistle. Unless we hear it, we stay here.'

'But—'

'And if you ask again, I'm going to take these reins and tie you up with them, OK?' Stef lifted the curtain with one finger and gave him a dirty look before letting it drop again.

Herc huffed. 'You know, just because you feel bad about being horrible to Joe, you don't have to take it out on me. Why have you been so weird lately, anyway?' Then in a small voice: 'You can talk to me about it, you know. I'm a good listener.'

Stef opened his mouth to deny it, but the words died in his throat. Herc was right. He *had* been weird, and he was suddenly overcome with a longing to talk to someone about it, to unburden himself. And it was somehow easier to talk to a disembodied voice, even if that voice was Herc's.

He took a long, shuddering breath, passed the reins over and under his fingers, and began to speak. It was all pouring out now and he couldn't stop it. He talked about growing up at St Halibut's – Miss Happyday's constant put-downs, the cruel gibes that slowly seeped into his mind and his heart and taught him that he was worthless. And then how he'd felt safe in St Halibut's once she'd gone and it was just them. He talked about how important Herc and Tig were to him, his own little family, but how lately he'd felt left out, acutely aware that they were siblings and put each other first. How he'd been unable to crack knitting, no matter how hard he tried, and everyone else seemed to feel settled and happy right away.

And then Benadrylla had come. 'And I thought I'd finally found something that was just right for me, something I could be good at. Something with a future. But it turned out to all be a big trick. Joke's on me, again.' He paused, half hoping that Herc would disagree, or at least mutter something reassuring. But the silence from the back spoke volumes. A tear leaked out and Stef knuckled it away, trying not to sniff too obviously. 'Anyway. Joe and I just got off on the wrong foot. When we see him again, I'll say sorry, all right?'

No answer.

'Herc?'

Suddenly the silence from the back seemed to have taken on a different quality. Stef turned, and twitched aside the curtain. The cart was empty. He jumped down and looked around. Herc was nowhere to be seen.

Stef couldn't tell how long he'd been alone, but he suspected it had begun very shortly after Herc suggested he start talking.

'Why, you devious little—'

❧ Chapter Twenty-Three ❧

Tig was starting to despair. Nellie had just returned and it wasn't good news – the staff door remained firmly shut and the footmen at the front entrance were greeting every official. There was no way they wouldn't notice a couple of scruffy kids trying to slip past. Besides that, the Palatial's row upon row of windows were shut tight, except for one on the fifth floor. There didn't even seem to be a fire escape. They were going to have to climb the drainpipe at the side of the building. It ran from the roof straight down to the ground. There was no ledge. No handholds. Nothing. But it did run next to the one open window. Ashna would have been up there in two shakes.

Tig could already feel the sweat making her hands slippery – not a good start. Then she dragged her eyes away from the drainpipe for the first time and did a double take at Nellie.

'Nell . . . what are you wearing? Where did you get that?'

Her friend was smoothing down a pink silk dress that was about six sizes too big for her, hoicking it up and tucking it into her knickers so that it didn't drag on the ground. A stylish matching pink hat framed her filthy face. 'Like it? You'd think the Head of Lost Property would know not to leave 'er luggage lyin' around, wouldn't you?'

'You won't be able to get up the drainpipe in that!' Nellie ignored her. 'Right, your turn.'

'Forget it. I'm not dressing up like that.'

'Course not,' Nellie told her. 'That would be daft. Nope, *this* is what *you're* wearin'.'

Before she could object, Nellie had pulled something over Tig's head. She looked down at herself. A servant's smock.

A horrible sense of dread crept through her.

'We're not going up the drainpipe?'

Nellie scoffed, plonking a cap on Tig's head and tying the ribbon straps under her chin. 'Don't be daft. You and me, we ain't Ashna. And there's, I dunno, a hundred bedrooms here. We don't 'ave time to fanny about. I'm gonna go and just ask 'em where 'e is.' She chuckled at Tig's horrified expression, then spat on her hands and rubbed them, considering her grubby fingernails with dissatisfaction. 'What this job calls for is a bit o' brass neck. You just follow and leave the talkin' to me.'

It was lucky, Herc thought, that he was the kind of boy who could think on his feet. Even when those feet were being pulled up to stand on their tiptoes by a large, white-aproned man who was bawling angrily into his face.

This had not been part of Herc's plan. He had been heading down the side of the building towards the towering stack of hay bales that were leaning against the side of the stables. A few short leaps and a little climb

188

would bring him on to its roof, from where he could listen to what was happening within. He'd know Pamela's bleat anywhere. And then he only had to make himself known to her – his own special bleat – and she'd break out to get to him. It might cause a bit of a palaver, but that wasn't a bad thing – it would distract attention from the main building, where Tig and Nellie were trying to find Joe. So, in a way, he was helping them.

Except now things had gone a bit wrong.

The first he'd known about it was when a voice had screeched, 'WHERE D'YOU THINK YOU'RE GOING?' by his right ear,

just as he was passing the staff entrance. 'Where's your uniform, toerag? Stop muttering. Just wear this one.'

He'd been dragged inside by his ear, and a bundle of clothes dumped into his arms, with a threat that if he wasn't wearing them ready for work in less than thirty seconds, he'd be buried in them instead.

Herc tugged at the red and gold waistcoat. The uniform was itchy, and smelt terrible, too – there was a faint whiff of lard wafting from the jacket, along with a strong stench of stale underarm. It was also far too big, and Herc had had to roll up the sleeves so thickly that he could barely bend his arms.

The kitchen was full of steam and harassed voices. A dozen other young staff members scurried around stirring pots and chopping vegetables and turning roasting meat over the fire. He'd been shoved towards a huge bag of onions and now could barely see through the stinging mist as he chopped. A large cage full of chickens clucked and fluttered on the floor by his feet, presumably destined for the pot. Although, as he blinked through the haze, he noticed that they weren't chickens. They were pigeons.

And not just any pigeons. The little tags round their legs marked them as Arfur's. How had *they* got here?

Like the master spy that he was, he observed, adapted, and made new plans. His uniform was the perfect disguise.

He could move freely around the hotel and the grounds now, without being questioned. All he had to do was find the right moment to slip out.

Fortunately, the chef was happy to help.

'You!' he thundered, pointing at Herc. 'Take that stew out and serve it. NOW!' He indicated a huge stockpot that was bubbling over the fire.

'Righto,' said Herc, turning round enthusiastically and dropping the knife to the floor. It narrowly avoided his foot and he picked it up, flicking the bar on the pigeons' cage as he did so. The door swung open slightly.

'It's up to you now,' he whispered to them. 'You're free! Go back to Arfur!'

The pigeons continued to coo and strut in circles. Maybe they really were stupid, after all.

As he stood back up, the chef snatched the knife from him with a curse and gave him a stinging belt around the ear with the other hand.

'Hurry up!' The chef yanked the pot off the stove with his meaty hands and handed it to Herc. He stumbled under its weight.

'Ow! It's hot!'

'And it better still be when you serve it,' the chef shot back. 'There's hungry ministers out there and if they're not happy I won't get paid, so don't make a mess of it.

Now go. Just stand there, and they can help themselves with the ladle. No, not like that! You need both hands to hold the pot.'

Herc grimaced as he heaved the stew down the corridor towards the dining hall. He glanced back to see the chef watching him. No chance of dumping the stew and running. He'd just have to serve it up as quickly as possible so he could get out to the stables to rescue Pamela.

The dining hall was awash with noise – one long table with chairs either side, diners talking loudly over one another. The first thing Herc saw was Benadrylla Crumplepatch seated on the far side, at the head of the table. He had a moment of panic, but she was talking to the woman on her left and paid no attention to him. Herc angled his face away just in case.

Everybody was eating and talking at the same time. For a bunch of people who cared so much about the correct order of bits of paper, they certainly didn't apply the same standards to table manners. Perhaps they had used up all their fussiness on everything else. Herc watched as a man whose lapel identified him as *Minister for Desk Tidying* explained to the bored-looking woman next to him how his pencil sharpeners were arranged, spraying crumbs over her every time he said 'sharpener'. The man turned and his eyes lit on Herc.

'Ah! What have you got there?'

Herc tried to assemble his features into a professional-waiter expression. 'It's stew.'

Desk Tidying frowned. 'Well, come here then and give me some. What kind of stew? Rabbit? Chicken? Beef? Llama?'

'Uh, dunno.'

The man leaned over and practically stuck his nose in the pot. 'Smells delicious. Venison, perhaps.' He took hold of the ladle. 'You there! What's the stew?' he shouted, past Herc's right ear, to one of the uniformed footmen nearby. The footman dipped his head politely. 'It's goat, sir. Chef's special. Very fresh.'

Time stopped.

The noise of talking, laughing and the clatter of cutlery on plates echoed round the hall.

But Herc could hear nothing except the pounding of blood in his head.

Goat stew.

His hands trembled violently and boiling liquid splashed up over his wrist. He felt nothing.

'Hey, watch it!' the minister yelled as a slop of it landed in his lap.

193

Pamela. What have they done to you?

He looked around the dining hall, dazed. Everyone continued eating and talking with their mouths full, and helping themselves to dishes on the table, eyes glinting with greed. He felt as though his guts, his heart, his lungs, everything, had turned to molten lava in an instant, a heat like nothing he had ever felt before, a pressure so great that if he so much as breathed, fire would shoot out and incinerate the whole world.

Tears tried to come but seemed stuck, somehow, burned up by sheer grief.

A monstrous power was building in him. The stockpot no longer seemed to have any weight to it, as though it might float away. Desk Tidying had returned the ladle to the pot and was tucking in to the mess on his plate, dribbling sauce down his chin and smacking his lips, as a waiter nudged Herc aside to refill glasses from a jug.

Herc could feel it surging inside him: an explosion was coming. And there was nothing he could do to stop it.

✎ Chapter Twenty-Four ✎

To be fair, Nellie timed it beautifully.

She stepped neatly around a huge, long-handled leather case that three of the footmen were gamely trying to haul up the grand steps to the entrance, and had almost made it through the large wooden double door that was being held open by the remaining footman, when he put out a hand to stop her.

'Why thank you, my good man!' Nellie said without breaking stride, in a voice so posh that Tig almost didn't believe it had come out of Nellie's mouth. The next thing that came out was a plum stone, which Nellie placed graciously in the footman's outstretched hand before sweeping past him into the building. The footman stared at the sticky mess on his glove, immediately occupied with the dilemma of how to get rid of the thing in a seemly manner. Tig stumbled after Nellie, tripping up the final step in her hurry and placing a muddy footprint on the trailing dress, which was already escaping its tucks.

Nevertheless, they were in.

The floor of the entrance hall was polished marble, so shiny you could see the reflection of the gilded ceiling patterns. The lights from the chandelier sparkled under Tig's feet as she walked, making her slightly dizzy. Were it not for the situation, she would have been tempted to give it a run-up and slide on her heels all the way to the reception desk.

When the receptionist looked up she had a perfect smile on her face and her lips opened in greeting, only for her expression to freeze as she took in the entirety of Nellie. Tig almost felt sorry for her. Nellie cut a small but formidable figure in her outsized dress. She held herself up, as far as her five-foot frame would allow, and exuded the complete and utter confidence that comes from a life of privilege, wealth and power. But the plum juice around her mouth and tangled hair tumbling from under the hat told a different story.

A battle seemed to rage within the receptionist – stuck between sucking up to an important official and calling Security to have her thrown out. She appeared to land somewhere in the middle.

'Yes?' she said carefully.

'Fenella Frenchfries-Andgravy,' Nellie announced. 'Hi

wish to freshen hup in my hroom.'

The receptionist's eyes flitted from left to right for help, but found none. She consulted the paper in front of her. 'Er, I . . . There's nobody of that name . . . I can't let you through, I'm afraid—'

Nellie recoiled as though stung. 'Good grief. Hi'll have you know I am *hextremely* senior in the government.'

The woman looked sceptical. 'You're in the Cabinet?'

'Don't be ridhiculous! Hi am right heeyah! Why would Hi be in a cupboard?' Nellie smoothed down her dress. 'There would be no FUN without meh! Where is Stapleford Pinch? I must see him himmediately.' She slapped her palm on the desk and the woman flinched. 'He will be furious hat this treatment of a verreh himportant member of his staff!'

A couple of glances were thrown curiously their way.

The woman's eyes widened in alarm. 'Please keep your voice down. Mr Pinch has already gone through to the dining hall.' She checked her papers again as though they might say something different this time. 'The meal is only for *senior* staff. And you're rather late.'

'A feast without Frenchfries-Andgravy? Never! Stop slouching, Polleh. Hif you hadn't been so slow polishing my diamonds, we'd have been here hearlier.'

Tig realized Nellie was talking to her and straightened

up. 'Sorry, ma'am. Please don't fire me. And don't get this nice lady fired either, like you did with that other hotel receptionist yesterday.' Then she muttered out of the side of her mouth to the woman. 'She's a nightmare, I tell you. Everywhere she goes, bang, bang, everyone drops like flies.'

The woman blanched. 'I . . . I'm sure we can work something out.'

Nellie sighed impatiently. 'What habout my very good friend, Benadrylla Crumplepatch? She will vouch for me. Send a message up to her hroom. Number . . .' Nellie waggled her fingers at her ear as though trying to remember. 'Forty-two? Forty-three?' Her voice was shrill and demanding.

'Sixty-five,' said the receptionist quickly, keeping her voice low in an effort to encourage Nellie to do the same. 'But Ms Crumplepatch is also already in the dining hall. Lunch is being served.'

'Then I demand to see your superiahh!' trilled Nellie. 'This instant! This mistake must be rectified before I miss the hluncheon!'

A flicker of uncertainty passed over the woman's face, then she nodded and slipped through a door behind the desk.

Without a moment's pause, Nellie leaned over and

plucked a key from the hook labelled *65* on the wall, dangling it in front of Tig's face.

'See?' she whispered. 'Sometimes you just 'ave to ask.'

✀ Chapter Twenty-Five ✀

There are some things that happen so fast, and are over so quickly, that nobody is sure of the exact sequence of events. All that is left are the results.

To Herc, however, in the agony of his grief, every movement was crystal clear.

He saw the waiter's face change from calm composure, through confusion, then shock, to pain as the stew pot landed on his foot, in its immaculately polished shoe. Herc saw the waiter's arms jerk, and the jug of wine he was holding rise into the air, high, higher, spinning, the liquid spiralling out in rosy droplets, a waterfall that cascaded over the head of the Minister for Desk Tidying and his nearest neighbour on the right, a red-haired woman whose lapel declared her to be Minister for Pie Charts, who was just about to bite into a dumpling. Desk Tidying roared and jumped to his feet, his elbow striking out, into the chest of Pie Charts, who promptly swallowed the dumpling whole and began to choke. Then, like a river meeting an obstacle, the action split into two tumbling streams.

On Desk Tidying's left, the Senior Minister for Paperclips screamed in horror at his only good tie having been splashed by stew. To *his* left, the Deputy Minister for Replacement Staples (Size 2) tried to helpfully dab at his neighbour's tie with the tablecloth, but in her enthusiasm pulled one of the candelabras along with it, which toppled to the floor and set light to the Minister for Ink and Erasers' velvet trousers.

Meanwhile, the quick-thinking waitress standing behind the choking Minister for Pie Charts leaped forward heroically, wrapped her arms around her, and gave an almighty squeeze, which freed the dumpling and sent it shooting at approximately sixty miles per hour across the table, where it hit the Assistant Minister for Box Ticking on the side of his head. The Assistant Minister for Box Ticking, being a somewhat intemperate fellow, immediately assumed that he had been attacked by his long-time rival, the Under-Secretary for Highlighting (Yellow), and swung a punch at him. *He*, however, had that very second dived across the table to save his plate of trifle, which had been unceremoniously removed from his grasp when the tablecloth had been yanked, and the punch sailed over his head, instead landing full force in the face of the hotel's head butler, who had stepped in to calm the situation. The butler saw a spectacular sunburst with sparkles at the edge of his vision, and then passed out, falling, like a mighty oak, face first into the gooseberry jelly.

At this moment there was what sounded like applause.

Heads (those that were not in a headlock) swivelled towards the open door, where the noise turned out to be caused by the flapping of wings of a couple of dozen birds, swooping clumsily out of the kitchen, down the corridor, and over the heads of the slack-jawed footmen.

Pigeons, in fact.

Finding themselves stuck in the great hall, the birds began to flutter aimlessly, perching on the picture rail, the grand mantelpiece, the candelabras, and various heads of officials. A slick of creamy brown muck slid down into the eyes of the Minister for Hole Punches as a grey pigeon made herself comfortable in his hair.

Around this time, the Minister for Alphabetization (A to C) noticed the fire spreading from the Minister for Ink and Erasers' velvet trousers, but, having spent so long in filing cabinets A to C, she could only remember vocabulary from this area and therefore spent half a minute trying to recall the appropriate word for the really hot incandescent flamey stuff created when you set light to something. 'C-conflagration! Conflagration!' she finally yelled triumphantly, gesticulating furiously at the trousers.

The Minister for Ink and Erasers looked down and, belatedly, the scent of his own burning leg-hair sent him into a wild panic; he whipped off the trousers and, screeching 'F-f-f-fire!' flung them across the table, where they landed in the rum punch. This gave the flames new vigour, sending up a spectacular fireball that scorched the ceiling and burned off the eyebrows of a secretary who had only started work in the Labels department the previous day, and didn't recall this being part of the job description. The ever-vigilant Minister for Paper Shredding grabbed the nearest jug of water and tossed it over the flames so enthusiastically that it not only put out the flames but soaked the Minister for Ring Binders from head to toe. He reacted by stumbling backwards and stepping on Herc's foot, causing him to cry out, frozen to the spot in grief and pain as the calamity unfolded in front of him.

Moments later, glass showered into the room as a window smashed. A flash of white leaped through it, knocking over three chairs and a deputy minister.

There was a sudden moment of quiet as everybody blinked to check that a goat really had just jumped through a window, eyes blazing, in search of the source of the cry she had heard. Even the pigeons stopped nodding and flapping. Then there was an ecstatic cry of 'Pamela!' and the goat's head whipped round to see Herc at the other end of the long table. A length of broken chain was affixed to her neck, and as she turned her head, it flew round and knocked out the Under-Secretary for Pencils. There was a malignant hostility in her eyes – she'd eaten no chamomile since the previous evening and her rage level was back up to 100 out of 10.

The goat gave an almighty leap on to the table, letting off a volley of furious bleats, hooves scrabbling across the slipping tablecloth, the chain whipping from side to side behind her, knocking over ministers like skittles. Cutlery and glasses, dishes and bottles, flew to all sides in her wake as she galloped. Pigeons rose up en masse out of her path, sending feathers spiralling into the air. Reaching the other end of the long table, Pamela skidded to a halt, not quite soon enough to avoid barrelling into the chef, who had just entered, proudly bearing his showstopping dessert, an enormous pavlova.

Herc, engulfing Pamela in a hug, missed the journey of the pavlova. It was too fast for anyone to react, or to halt its inexorable progress in an arc through the air, or to change its fate, which was to land, cream side first, on the face of Benadrylla Crumplepatch. It slid down in a meringuey, creamy, fruity mess, clinging lovingly to her skin and her blonde ringlets, the rest of it dropping dismally into her silken lap.

'Never mind, everyone,' Herc said happily into the silence that fell, his desperation and misery gone so suddenly that it was hard to believe they had ever been there at all. 'Found her! Found my goat, after all.' He paused, considering the room, and added politely, 'Hope I didn't interrupt.'

❧ Chapter Twenty-Six ❧

Room 65 was on the second floor. Both girls put their ears to the door but could hear nothing. A quick glance each way down the corridor: no one. The pink dress and the servant's smock lay in a crumpled heap where they had thrown them. Quickly Nellie put the key in the lock and tried to turn it. It wouldn't go.

She frowned. Was it the wrong key? She took it out and checked – *65* was engraved on it. She tried the handle, and was so taken by surprise when it turned easily that she stumbled into the room.

Joe was standing a few feet away, looking out of the window. He whirled round as they came in, astonished. 'N-Nellie? Tig?'

'It weren't even locked! Didn't you try the door?'

It took a few seconds before he found the ability to speak. 'I didn't . . . no, I . . . I just assumed . . . What on earth are you doing here?'

Tig laughed. 'Rescuing you, of course! We were so worried!'

Nellie was less sympathetic. 'Gordon Bennett, you could have just walked out! What a muppet.'

Joe appeared to be in shock and merely blinked at them. Perhaps Benadrylla had drugged him?

Tig took charge of the situation. 'Come on.' She took his hand and tried to drag him from the room. 'We're going to walk right down there, and Cuthbert's going to tell the Head Minister for FUN what's been going on. Maisie's looking after Ashna because she's ill, otherwise she'd be here, too. So walk tall, confirm what happened. Then we're out of here. Stef and Herc are outside waiting with the cart.'

Nellie grabbed his other arm impatiently, but he just stared at her as she yanked it practically out of its socket.

'Wait,' he said. 'I need to tell you something.'

Nellie tugged him again towards the door. 'Not now – we need to move.'

But he wouldn't budge; he looked suddenly sick. 'It's . . . it's too dangerous. Go without me. Now. Quick. I never thought you'd actually come.'

Nellie's fingers itched to slap the nonsense out of him. *Definitely* drugged. 'Mate, please. You're not thinking straight.'

He shook his head. 'You don't understand. She said you'd come. I didn't think you would, but—' He broke off. He didn't seem anywhere near as happy as he ought to be. 'You shouldn't have—'

Nellie, losing patience, pivoted behind him and gave him a hefty shove towards the door.

Right into the arms of three security guards.

It was as though the guards knew they'd be coming. Stef had taken no more than ten steps from the cart when he was challenged by two men in Crumplepatch Railways uniforms, who seemed to spring from nowhere. They frogmarched him into the hotel where his heart sank to see Cuthbert being held between two of the hotel staff, having been dragged out from bushes underneath the window of the dining room, where he'd been trying to catch snatches of FUN conversation. Just when he'd thought it couldn't get worse, there was a commotion on the wide stairs leading into the foyer: Tig, Nellie and Joe were being shoved down them, struggling.

'We demand to see Stapleford Pinch,' Cuthbert was yelling. 'We have important information for him.'

'Oh you'll see him, all right,' said one of the guards. 'But it's Ms Crumplepatch that wants you.'

They were all shoved through the door of the dining

room into a scene of chaos.

The guards seemed taken aback – it hadn't looked like this earlier – and loosened their grip on the children.

No minister or official was unscathed. Some of them appeared to be unconscious, one or two were weeping, others sat in shock. Several were groaning and clutching their heads. The table was a pile of shards of china and glass and sausage rolls on top of smashed chocolate roulade and gherkins. People were trying to wring custard out of their clothes, and slipping as they stepped over each other. Pamela was grazing on an upended bowl of green salad, pausing only to headbutt a brave minister who tried to shoo her away, sending him sprawling into Stapleford Pinch's lap. Trifle and pavlova dripped from the chandelier while a pigeon tried to hold onto it upside down to catch the drips in its beak.

At the end of the table stood Benadrylla, who looked as though she'd been dusted with flour, dragged through a vat of breadcrumbs, feathered, and then dunked in a bucket of mixed puddings. There was nothing sweet about her expression, though. If looks could kill, not a single person would be left alive.

Tig's eye lit on Herc, nuzzling Pamela's neck while she finished off the salad. His clothing was in a similar state to Benadrylla's.

'Herc! Are you all right?'

He grinned on seeing her.

'It's OK! Pamela's fine. They didn't cook her!'

Tig wasn't sure where to start.

'THERE THEY ARE!' Benadrylla's voice thundered round the room. There was a hush, apart from the sound of muffled sobs coming from the Minister for Alphabetization (A to C) somewhere under a table.

'Found these kids, just like you said,' offered one of the guards, having decided the only way forward was to pretend everything was normal.

'These . . . urchins are responsible for this outrage,' Benadrylla said, pausing to wipe pavlova from her eye. 'They have attempted to thwart the railway at every turn, and now they attack FUN itself!'

Every eye turned on them. Stapleford Pinch was regarding them with confusion. Tig's heart thudded in her chest. She nodded at Cuthbert – there was only one thing for it: the truth.

'Thank you for seeing us,' Cuthbert said cordially, as though they had arrived for an appointment. 'Mr Pinch, sir. We came to inform you of illegal activity that has been going on under your very nose. Benadrylla Crumplepatch . . . is a criminal!' There were gasps around the room, from those who still had enough breath. 'She kidnapped our friend here. And as I'm sure you know, that is not only in contravention of the highest laws of this land but –' he paused before adding the real clincher – 'I think you will find he was transported here without a seatbelt.'

There was a scream, and then a thud, as an official keeled over.

Tig gestured at Joe. 'It's true. She took Joe here, and kept him against his will!'

FUN mouths were open in shock all round the room.

'Can this be true?' Pinch asked Benadrylla, digging out some apple crumble from his ear. 'Surely not. If there has been any illegal—'

'It's nonsense!' She waved dismissively. 'A ridiculous accusation cooked up to divert attention from their crimes.'

'It's true!' Herc piped up. 'Joe, tell them! Tell them how those people grabbed you in the middle of the night! AND she stole Pamela!'

For some reason, Benadrylla was smirking. 'Yes, *Joe*, do tell them.'

'Go on,' urged Tig.

Joe dredged up a long, shaky breath and glanced at Herc before dropping his gaze. 'Ms Crumplepatch didn't kidnap me.'

Nellie whipped round in wide-eyed disbelief. 'He's confused. She must have threatened him,' she told the room, before hissing at Joe, 'You've got to tell them! You're the proof!'

Joe shook his head, his eyes shut tight. Benadrylla sighed impatiently. 'After your unlawful activities in my camp, I instructed Joe to befriend you in order to report back, and he removed the goat before leaving because it is – as you can clearly see – a dangerous animal.'

Herc began to tremble, arms encircling Pamela's neck.

'No,' breathed Tig, horror creeping across her face.

Stef's face was bloodless. 'So I was right? Joe . . . You're her *spy?*'

Joe now seemed incapable of looking at any of them.

Benadrylla, however, was smiling. 'Oh, he's no mere spy.' She waited, eyebrows raised expectantly.

Finally Joe's voice came in a low mutter. 'I'm her son.'

The FUN officials had retreated to their rooms to get cleaned up, and the hotel staff began the unenviable task of setting the dining hall to rights, opening all the windows and attempting to chivvy out the pigeons, who were far more interested in helping clear up the cake crumbs stuck in the ceiling fan.

The children found themselves locked in the hotel's wine cellar, despite Cuthbert's protests that they were too young to be anywhere near alcohol.

It would have been easier to split an atom than to detach Pamela from Herc right now – she had made it clear what she thought about that idea by barging one of the guards through three sets of wine racks and pinning him to the floor – so she had been left in the cellar along with them. Somehow Pamela seemed to have escaped any injury from the breaking glass; there was not even a smudge on her pristine white hair.

She was much calmer now, not only for having been reunited with Herc, but also because of the large bunches of chamomile from Stef's pockets, which she was working her way through, sighing heavily every now and then.

'Hey, if you keep her away from that stuff maybe she can break us out of here,' suggested Nellie. 'This is one time we could use her temper.'

'She's not a weapon, you know,' said Herc, outraged. She's got feelings. We're not going to upset her just because it's useful.' He ran his fingers through her neck hair reassuringly.

'Also,' Stef pointed out, 'that's a solid oak door, not some tumbledown old shed. There's no way even she can break that down.'

After that, they spoke little, the only noises the parps of Pamela's farts and the clink of bottles as Herc tried to play tunes on them with his shoes.

An hour later, Benadrylla came to see them, along with a couple of Crumplepatch goons, though she left them waiting outside the closed door of the cellar. Joe skulked behind her; clearly, he had been forced to come along but was trying to keep as much distance between himself and the orphans as possible. His mother had washed all trace of the feast from herself, and was instead dripping with diamonds – earrings, necklace and shimmering rings. She wore a clean new blue dress covered in pansies. Pamela considered it for a moment, but appeared to decide the chamomile was tastier.

Herc launched himself at Joe, pummelling him ineffectually. 'You took Pamela! You were going to let them eat her! I thought you were my friend!'

Pamela merely stood and watched, chewing. Tig would never understand her. No matter how relaxed she was feeling now, if Pamela were as loyal and loving as Herc made out, she'd surely have unleashed some of her wrath on Benadrylla, and not just a few blobs of food: if anyone was crying out for a goat bite on the bum, it was that woman.

Joe made no attempt to defend himself, merely covering his face with his hands while Herc's small fists landed on his stomach. 'I'm sorry,' he sobbed. 'I didn't mean for . . . I didn't realize you . . .'

His mother observed them with a disgusted air. 'Oh, please. You did what needed to be done, Joe. Don't be such a baby about it now.'

Stef stepped forward and gently pulled Herc away, enveloping him in a hug.

'I expect you're wondering what I plan to do with you,' Benadrylla said, turning her attention back to the orphans.

'Nope.' Nellie jutted out her chin. 'If you think it's evil

speech time, go and give it to someone who cares, like the mirror. And by the way, you're not allowed to keep us in here.'

'Wrong. You were caught trespassing on the hotel's property and causing a disturbance.'

'She's right,' Cuthbert told them gloomily. 'Legally, we can be held temporarily in a secure area until such time as we can be processed by the authorities.'

Benadrylla beamed. 'And now that you've been *entirely* humiliated and discredited in public, it only remains for me to rub it in your faces tomorrow at the opening ceremony. I'm holding it in the clearing – thank you *so* much for vacating it, by the way. Finnick would have been awkward if you had still been there, but since it was abandoned he had no choice but to watch my machines roll right over your pathetic little huts. I've had word – it's all done and dusted now.'

The children absorbed the news, imagining the axes and crushing machines at work on Marshmallow.

'I don't understand,' Tig told her. 'You weren't allowed to. The map . . .'

She laughed. 'Things change. You'll see for yourself tomorrow. And after that, you will be working for me in my coal mine. Bickley said the best place for you all is down a deep, dark, pit. Happily, I own one.'

217

'Mr Brimstone?' Herc said, indignant. 'You shouldn't listen to him. Ashna says he's hypnotizing people. He's probably done it to you, too. Maybe that's why you're being so evil.'

At this, Joe tugged at his mother's sleeve, alarmed. 'Mum, do you think he might have—?'

Benadrylla laughed. She laughed so much that tears came into her eyes. 'Oh, that's funny. It really is. As if *Bickley* could hypnotize anyone! That man's vendetta against you all has been useful, in a small way, but he has a vastly inflated sense of his own abilities and importance. It is I who pull the strings. I always have.'

'Either way,' countered Cuthbert. 'You can't touch us. We're adopted, now. You'd have to get our father's permission to send us down the mine, and he'd never give that.'

'But your so-called father abandoned you.' Benadrylla blinked innocently. 'Where is he, hmm? It's been pointed out to the authorities that he has not been seen anywhere near you the entire time. It's one thing to be playing alone in the woods, another to be living there without an adult.'

'He hasn't abandoned us!' cried Stef – though as he spoke, he remembered his and Ashna's last conversation with Arfur. It did not fill him with confidence.

Benadrylla scoffed. 'Bickley tells me *your dad* couldn't

care less. I assume you know that he was *paid* when he adopted you? DEATH provide compensation when orphans are taken off their hands, you see.'

She saw from their faces that they hadn't known. Her laugh tinkled around the cellar again.

'You didn't think he did it out of the goodness of his heart, did you? Oh, how precious! Never mind. I have graciously offered to take care of you all myself.'

The children stared back at her, their hearts in their shoes.

'You're mine, now.'

Chapter Twenty-Seven

shna turned miserably in her sheets, all alone, Maisie having moved into the dormitory with the Poppets for now. The Mending House Guvnor might be under Bickley Brimstone's influence, but it seemed he had not yet managed to squash her kind nature.

Ashna felt a little stronger physically, though her chest ached from the flare-up of her lungs and the terrible news from the Palatial.

Word had reached Maisie – via her niece, a cleaner at the hotel – of the day's events: Joe's betrayal, her friends' capture. And the destruction of Marshmallow was confirmed. According to Maisie's niece, listening to the FUN officials gossiping, the clearing had been flattened, and all trace of their hard work crushed. Instead, the tracks now met in the middle and Crumplepatch Railways workers were setting up a small stage and chairs ready for the ceremony tomorrow. She had not been able to find out what had happened to the orphans – only that they were in trouble. Nobody could find Arfur, last seen heading out to the dump with more books. The skies were silent and empty without his pigeons.

Sleep eluded Ashna, her brain spiralling desperately for a way to save them all. She listened to the pouring summer rain outside, a solid stream from the night sky as if it were trying to drown Sad Sack, and the skittering and scratching of mice along the walls as they sheltered from the deluge.

Then a rattle above her head made her sit bolt upright. She was pretty sure mice couldn't throw stones. In the old days of the Mending House the windows had been barred and locked, but now that no one wanted to escape, Maisie had replaced them with sliding panes.

Ashna stood up stiffly on the bed, opened the window, and poked her head out. A dark figure turned his pale face up to her wordlessly. Swallowing her shock, she dragged her leaden limbs round to the gate – quietly, so as not to waken Maisie – and let the visitor in.

She didn't say anything for a few minutes after Joe had finished speaking. They had talked in the courtyard, the rain gradually soaking them through, to avoid waking anyone.

221

Finally Ashna found her voice. 'You *what?*'

He turned his dark eyes on her. 'I want you to help my mother.'

'So I heard that, um, your mum is, y'know . . . Benadrylla Crumplepatch,' Ashna pointed out tactfully.

'Yes.'

'You're Joe Crumplepatch.'

His mouth twisted awkwardly. 'She doesn't like me to use her surname, or let on that we're related when we're on site. Says I don't deserve it yet. But . . . yes.'

It was certainly an unexpected development.

Everything about Joe suggested he was telling the truth. He'd driven Bernard on the post cart ten miles back to Sad Sack through the night's rain. And there was no other possible reason for him to approach the very person who had most reason to hate him. He'd even brought back Arfur's pigeons, to prove he meant it. They cooed and flapped as he released them from the cage at his feet, and the two of them watched the birds snuggle into their coop. 'Your friends – and Pamela – are all locked in the hotel cellar,' he told Ashna apologetically. 'Guarded.'

'We should have listened to Stef,' Ashna muttered. 'We thought he was just jealous.' She crossed her arms over her chest angrily. No matter how sorry he was, it wasn't enough.

Joe made no attempt to argue. He admitted he'd been jealous of Stef, who seemed to do no wrong in his mother's eyes, and was everything she wished Joe was . . . until it turned out she couldn't wrap him around her finger as she'd thought. 'It was my chance to please her. I've always been a disappointment to her, you see. I was supposed to sneak out last night and make it seem like there'd been a struggle so you'd come and rescue me. Except . . . I'd decided that I didn't want to do it. You guys had been good to me – including Stef, even. He tried to protect me from the cows' stampede, even though I'd been awful to him. I was going to stay. I thought if I stood up to her for once, maybe we could . . . I don't know.' He sighed, frustrated.

'But when you didn't come out, she sent her goons in to get you,' Ashna guessed.

He nodded miserably. 'She always gets what she wants. But she's never done anything as bad as this before.' Joe licked his lips nervously. 'And something Herc said got me thinking. What if it's not her fault she's been behaving like this? What if Bickley Brimstone's hypnotized her? If we can find out what he's doing and stop it, she might come to her senses.'

'Joe . . .' Ashna shook her head in irritation. 'It sounds like your mum has been . . . well, not a nice person for quite a while.'

'But she's worse, I'm sure of it,' he said desperately. 'She's always been ambitious and ruthless, but not . . . like this. Please. Let's go to Powders 'n' Potions right now and see what we can find. I know you'll be able to break in.'

It was tempting. She really *did* want to know once and for all what Bickley Brimstone was doing. But . . . 'Hang on. This could be another trick. How do I know you're not setting me up, Joe? Just like you set Stef up. You made us all think you were on our side.'

Joe sagged, hanging his head. 'I know you don't trust me, and I don't blame you. But I'm asking, I'm . . . begging you to help me.' He reddened. 'And it's the only way to stop your friends being sent to the coal mine in Rankshire.'

At this, Ashna straightened, shock coursing through her. 'Sent *where*?'

❧ Chapter Twenty-Eight ❧

Ashna felt a familiar squirm of excitement in her belly as she dropped from the ground-floor window at the side of Powders 'n' Potions to the floor of the back room. She closed it behind her, silently.

It had been a while since she'd done a proper break-in.

Back when she'd burgled for the wicked Mending House owner Ainderby Myers, she'd always felt bad about it. The victims were rich, but that didn't mean they deserved to lose their possessions, especially to a scumbag like him. Bickley Brimstone wasn't as wealthy as many of her previous victims had been, but she wasn't here to steal from him, anyway.

She had sent Joe back to the hotel. Benadrylla expected him to come with her to the ceremony the following day, and if he wasn't back in plenty of time it would arouse suspicion. Besides, this was one job she had always preferred to do alone.

It was her friends' only hope. Joe had said they were unlikely to last long at the coal mines in Rankshire. 'So many accidents . . .' It didn't bear thinking about.

The room was relatively bare – the walls were painted a dull grey and bore framed posters advertising various remedies sold in the shop beyond. Incense stood in a pot on the floor, cool and unlit. On the table stood a large china teapot decorated with blue swirls and a single cup in the same design, an open bag of tea next to it. Since the tea had been dried and crushed into flakes, it was impossible to tell exactly what plant it was. She held it a short distance from her nose and sniffed warily. It smelt a lot like chamomile. Her foot nudged a cardboard box tucked under the table. Opening it, she found it was full of plants.

She grabbed a handful. *Definitely* chamomile: a sunny, plump and dense disc at the centre, surrounded by pure white petals, much like a daisy, but with delicate frond-like leaves. She was certain, because it was all over the clearing at Marshmallow and she had double-checked it was safe to eat when Pamela showed such interest in it.

There was nothing special about this tea. Was the dodgy stuff being kept somewhere else?

She slumped into the cushioned chair to think and banged her leg painfully. Rubbing her knee, she noticed that there was a drawer set into the side of the table; the metal handle was what had hurt her.

She pulled experimentally on it. Locked. Not a problem.

Removing a short length of wire from a seam in her sleeve, she pushed it into the lock just under the handle, closed her eyes and allowed the end to stroke the inside gently until it found a crack. A jiggle, a click, and it was open.

The only object in the drawer was a large book, well thumbed, the cover nearly falling off. Interesting. It was a mighty thick and weighty tome for a man who had persuaded Arfur to get rid of all the books in the library.

The Secrets of Hypnotism.

Well, well, well. This must be the book Ma Yeasty had mentioned.

Lifting it out with both hands, she grimaced at the weight and it slipped out of her grip on to the table with a thump, making the china rattle noisily.

She held her breath and listened for any movement upstairs, but there was none.

Calming her racing heart, she opened to the contents page and began to read.

Hours later, eyes stinging, bottom sore and legs stiff, she reached the end of the final page and sat back, exhausted.

Through the grubby window the black night had turned grey. Time to go.

She stood up, muscles protesting, and returned the book to its drawer just as the door that led upstairs opened.

Brimstone's spindly figure loomed in the frame, wearing a nightshirt and cap, holding a steaming metal pot by a long handle. He stopped in surprise and blinked, before getting a hold of himself.

'What a coincidence!' he said, placing the pot on the table and locking the door behind him. 'I heard all about your friends' antics at the Palatial. I must say, they really did make fools of themselves in the most spectacular manner. Just as you are now. *Burglar.*'

Ashna's skin felt clammy. Sad Sack had no police force. Brimstone had never liked her or her friends. And now he had the perfect excuse: defending himself from a break-in.

She cursed herself for closing the window, and tensed to make a run for the door to the shop, but he was already there. The lock clicked; he pocketed the key.

'I see your hands are empty. Naturally, I do not keep much money in the shop – to do so would be foolhardy around here. You will have had a long and fruitless search for valuables. You must be tired.'

He turned back to face her, slowly.

'Tea, my dear?'

'No, thanks.'

He chuckled. 'Come come, you simply *mustn't* leave until you've tried it.' He poured hot water into the teapot and slid it across the table.

Behind him, the clock ticked, ticked, ticked.

With no other options, she sat, stiffly.

'I will tell you how this is going to work, Ashna,' he said. 'I'm very glad you're here, actually, because you can be my assistant tomorrow at the ceremony. I'm going to give a speech to the entire Ministry of FUN. And after it they will be putty in my hands, just like everyone else in Sad Sack.'

'You've been practising hypnotism on them,' she said warily. 'But you can't possibly hypnotize a whole crowd at once. It's not possible.'

A flash of irritation crossed his features. 'Of course I can. This has been my plan from the very start. Why did you think I was so keen on the railway? I knew it would bring FUN here. DEATH will no doubt send a few officials, too – they can't bear to be left out. I have been refining my technique over and over, until it's perfect. Just ask Ma Yeasty. Did you know it was she who informed me that you were all living up there alone, that Miss Happyday had died and you were covering it up?'

Ashna's blood turned to ice. 'Ma Yeasty?'

'Yes!' He chuckled at her expression. 'She didn't mean to. She felt so relaxed, and it just slipped out. You see, everyone is powerless in the face of my mentalist expertise. No one will be able to resist tomorrow! Even Ms Crumplepatch, oh-so-superior Benadrylla . . . I know she's been laughing at me. Well, she won't be laughing tomorrow. She'll see I'm her equal, and she'll be *begging* to work with me. I'll be in charge of FUN before the day is out. And I won't stop there. FUN, then DEATH, then . . . who knows? I might become Prime Minister. President. *Emperor* has a nice ring to it.'

'Wow. You seem to have it all sewn up,' Ashna admitted. 'But what makes you think I'm going to help?'

'Oh, you will.' He beamed. Behind him, the clock sang out its chirpy little six-note tune.

Ashna sighed deeply. It had been a long night. Her very bones ached with tiredness. Her throat was dry and scratchy.

'I think I'll have that tea, now,' she said, taking the cup in both hands. What was the harm? It was only chamomile.

It was warm, and soothing. So soothing.

✂ Chapter Twenty-Nine ✂

The transformation of Marshmallow was complete.

There was no trace of the huts. Their careful handiwork had been crushed, broken and removed overnight. In its place the entire Ministry of FUN were seated in rows, murmuring among themselves as they waited for proceedings to begin. A temporary wooden stage had been set up at one end. The final piece of the tracks had been lowered into position and fixed close to the spring, a pump ready for the driver to fill up from. The engine that Stef had so admired sat quietly on top, green metal gleaming. They had heard it coming before they saw it – the *puff-puff* of steam forced out under pressure; slowly it had drawn up to the water stop with a final sigh as it yielded to its brakes.

Tig, Stef, Herc, Nellie and Cuthbert were gathered at the back where they couldn't cause a nuisance but had a good view of the whole scene. A couple of

Benadrylla's goons stood by, leaning against a DEATH carriage, watching their every move. Finnick bustled around straightening chairs, looking utterly miserable. Pamela, at the end of a sturdy rope tied to a tree, was happily munching at weeds. The hotel had refused to let Benadrylla leave her there, and so it had been decreed that she would be let loose in the woods once they were all safely away, like the wild creature she so clearly was.

'At least they don't seem to have caught Ashna,' offered Stef, desperately searching for a bright side. 'Maisie's probably hiding her.'

'Spoke too soon,' Nellie told him, pointing.

Brimstone was swaggering on to the stage, clearing his throat and testing his voice. 'Me, me, me, me-me-me-me-me-me-me-mee!' he trilled. Behind him, silent, passive, stood Ashna.

'She doesn't look well.' Cuthbert frowned.

It was true. Ashna's body was slumped, leaning slightly to one side like a broken puppet.

'Hey, Ashna!' Herc yelled. 'Ashna! Over here!' Several FUN officials turned, frowned, *shhhh*ed. There was no response from their friend, though she must have heard.

Benadrylla strode over to them. 'That's enough of that. Any more noise and my guards will put you straight in that carriage where no one can see what's happening to you. Understand? If I were you, I'd enjoy the fresh air while you can.'

'Mum . . .' Joe had followed behind her, and now grabbed her arm.

Nellie screwed up her nose as though smelling something rotten. 'Oh, look who it is. Mummy's boy. Ain't you told enough tales on us yet?'

Joe reddened, but ignored her and clung to Benadrylla. 'Please. Just let them go – they won't bother you anymore. You've got your railway, haven't you? And . . . I think you should see a doctor or something about what Brimstone's done to you. See what he's done to Ashna? It's hypnotism, Mum. I'm worried about you.'

Benadrylla rounded on him so quickly and with such venom that he shrank back. 'Stop *embarrassing* me with your ridiculous ideas. Now everyone knows you're my son, I want you out of sight at all times, got it?'

'Please—'

But then there were three sharp claps from the stage and Brimstone's voice rose above the crowd. The murmuring quietened. He stared out at them all, Ashna in the shadows behind him.

'Shall we begin?'

★

234

Bickley had spent hours perfecting the programme for the ceremony and had paid a hefty sum for the calligraphy and copying. These things were important – start as you mean to go on, and all that. His reign over FUN was going to be top quality, like everything else he did. As he prepared to go on stage, he had run his fingers over the thick cream card and smiled to himself.

OPENING CEREMONY
Sad Sack to Little Wazzock Railway

Tea and Biscuits

A Short Speech of Welcome by
Bickley Brimstone, President*

A few words from Benadrylla Crumplepatch
of Crumplepatch Industries

The Cutting of the Ribbon by Stapleford Pinch,
currently Head Minister for FUN

FUN Celebrations

Carriages

*(of the Sad Sack Business Association)

He hadn't been able to resist putting 'currently' before Stapleford Pinch's job. He didn't care if Pinch noticed; it was too late. There would be only one speech: his. And when the time came for carriages, he'd be the only one celebrating. None of them would be able to look down on him anymore.

Not everyone had accepted his offer of tea, but it didn't matter. It was only one element of his hypnotic method. Hypnotism was easier at home in his back room, with the incense and the clock and his special mellifluous voice which helped people to relax; but his skill at mental manipulation was now so great that merely one or two of those elements would suffice. By the end of his short speech, every single person in the crowd would be under his spell. He was delighted to see that DEATH had sent a few officers, too, unwilling to let FUN have all the fun. He suppressed a giggle of excitement, sensing the expectation from the crowd in front of him.

He felt a nudge and turned to see Ashna holding the clock from his study, just as he had instructed her. He enjoyed the moment; he'd always wanted an assistant – without having to pay one – and it was particularly delicious that it was one of those sneering orphans who had disrespected him for so long. She'd only sneer now if he told her to.

The clock chimed its strange little tune. There were a

few bemused frowns from the audience. Someone asked, 'Is that the lunch bell?'

Ashna leaned forward and whispered something in his ear.

He began.

'I am delighted that you are all here to celebrate the grand opening of the Sad Sack to Little Wazzock rail line. It has been a long and difficult project, but thanks to my own genius, I can now announce that I am a complete fraud.'

There was a beat of silence, and one or two heads jerked up from where they had been gently dropping off to sleep. Benadrylla, standing to the side waiting for him to shut up so she could make *her* speech, looked half amused, half confused.

Bickley frowned, coloured and cleared his throat. 'Apologies. I meant to say of course that I have been working day and night to ensure that I end up in charge of FUN, and then the entire government. Arghh!' He clamped a hand over his own mouth.

Stapleford Pinch half rose to his feet. 'I beg your pardon? What is the meaning of this?'

The blood had drained from Bickley's head and he felt dizzy. The words coming from his mouth seemed to have no relation to what he'd planned. He stammered, 'No –

I . . . Hold on a minute.' He snatched his crib notes from Ashna and started again. 'I meant to say, of course, that I've been pretending to cure people and tell their fortunes, but that's all nonsense. I was secretly practising hypnotism so that I could take my revenge on you all.'

'Do you take us for fools?' cried a woman from the back, the Minister for Rubber Bands.

'Yes! I mean, nnnneurghhh!' gasped Bickley. 'I take you for . . . for . . . gnnh . . . gnnnhh!' His face was twisting and writhing as though a truth monster were trying to escape. 'I sssss . . . . set fire to St Halibut's. Burned it to the ground!'

Benadrylla now appeared deeply uncomfortable. He knew far too much about her own activities to be in such a confessional mood. She turned to the Head Minister for FUN. 'Pinch, remove him so that we can get on with signing off the railway.'

Pinch nodded, and was opening his mouth to give the appropriate orders when Bickley pointed directly at Benadrylla. He promptly grabbed his traitorous finger with his other hand, trying to shove it back down. It wouldn't go. 'And as for *her*,' he said. 'You won't believe what she's been up to.'

Benadrylla froze. 'Shut up, you berk! What are you doing?'

But Bickley was unstoppable. 'I'm explaining how you faked the paperwork, Ms Crumplepatch. You know, when you forced Hildegaard Hillfinger of Hubbashire to make a new map and used it to get permission to clear this place, because the children's huts were in the way. Then you got rid of Professor Hildegaard. Permanently.'

Gasps rose from the dignitaries. Benadrylla had turned beetroot-red and her eyes flicked from side to side in panic.

A man from Stamps and Permissions began screaming uncontrollably and had to be carried off.

'Stop, you fool!' screeched Benadrylla, dropping all effort at calmness. 'You're ruining everything!' She was on her feet, appealing to Stapleford Pinch. 'Get him away. He's deranged.'

Ashna, who had suddenly lost her broken-puppet slump, walked forward next to Bickley. 'Nope. He's telling the truth. Just like I told him to.'

'You told me to?' Bickley looked wild. 'I don't remember that.'

Ashna nudged the pharmacist away from centre stage and addressed the assembly. 'Last night, Bickley tried to hypnotize me, too. The thing is . . . he didn't count on me having read his hypnotism book – all the way to the end. And unlike him I didn't skip bits, so I learned how to do it *properly*. All I had to do was say a secret keyword just before he went on stage and he now has the most incredible urge to tell you everything, with complete honesty. Watch.'

The faces of the crowd turned from Ashna to Bickley and back again, mouths agape like baby birds waiting to be fed.

'Hey, Bickley, tell them what you really think of them.'

The pharmacist shook his head furiously but found

240

himself yelling, 'I think they're a bunch of—'

His next words were so incredibly rude that two officials from Appropriate Language fainted dead away. At a signal from Pinch, several secretaries rose from their seats and took hold of Bickley. He was shouting from between his fingers, apparently unable to stop himself. 'I've always despised you, Pinch! You don't deserve to be in charge of a single paperclip! It should be *my* picture on FUN headed paper! There should be statues of *me* in the town – I demand to be a figure of FUN! It's all I've ever wanted!'

'What's he saying?' asked a minister at the back.

Her neighbour shrugged. 'He's saying he just wants to have FUN.'

'Well, can't he do it without insulting everybody?'

Stapleford Pinch rose to his feet, trembling with anger. 'I think we've heard quite enough,' he thundered. 'Take that man away. And Crumplepatch –' he marched up to Benadrylla – 'this allegation of faked paperwork is *most* concerning.'

'And that's just what it is,' she snapped back. 'An *allegation*. You have no proof that I went anywhere near the mapmaker. Only the ravings of that fool.'

Pinch glanced hopefully around at his ministers in case any of them could solve this for him. Nobody spoke up.

'You can't touch me,' Benadrylla panted, 'because you can't prove a thing! None of you! It's all . . . Will you get *off* me, you vile creature!' This last was directed at Pamela, who had been happily chewing away on the marigolds of her dress for the past few minutes. 'Raaaaaaaah!'

She yanked the fabric, and the dress tore most of the way around the pocket where the goat's teeth remained firm. Something fell to the ground from the ripped pocket, and Pinch picked it up. A small velvet bag. When he pulled it open, two objects glinted in the dappled sunlight, a shimmer of gold and diamonds. 'What are these?'

Finnick scuttled over and peered at the objects in Pinch's fingers. 'Why, those are the celebrated calipers and compass of Hildegaard Hillfinger of Hubbashire!'

Benadrylla stuttered, 'She . . . she gave them to me. To make into jewellery! She didn't . . . didn't want them anymore.'

But Finnick wasn't having it. 'She would never have been parted from those, unless something terrible had happened to her! I knew it. I knew something was amiss with that map!'

For the first time, Benadrylla seemed lost for words.

Stapleford Pinch's expression was severe. 'This suggests strongly to me that you have committed contemptible and illegal acts. Who here can tell me if this evidence constitutes criminal proof? You there!' He called upon the Minister for Alphabetization (A to C) sitting in the front row. '"Crimes" falls into your filing cabinet. This is proof, is it not?'

The minister shot to her feet. 'Correct. If the clothing compartment just contained the compass I couldn't call her a cut-throat – that would be conjecture – but the crux of the case is that, collectively, the confession of the chemist, and, crucially, the calipers and compass, conclusively confirm this calamity: that Crumplepatch croaked the cartographer. I concur.'

'She seriously needs to move on to D to F,' muttered someone in the row behind.

'DEATH!' cried Stapleford Pinch. 'Take these criminals away.' The lounging officers sprang to attention, delighted to finally have something to do.

'No!' Bickley was yelling as he was bundled away to the DEATH carriage. 'I haven't finished yet! I need to tell you that none of the remedies I sell in the pharmacy work! They're all rubbish! I short-change everyone! I don't wash my hands after using the toilet! I pick my nose and wipe it under the counter! There are bogeys more than twenty years old there!'

His rants faded away as the carriage door slammed closed. Then it opened again to receive a shell-shocked, unresisting Benadrylla – and Joe, who it seemed would have to travel with his mother. For one short moment, Joe stared back at the orphans sadly, before being nudged roughly inside. Soon the vehicle was trundling away at speed along the cleared corridor of trees, alongside the shining rails, presumably destined for DEATH HQ.

There was a loud bleat, and the orphans turned to their unlikely saviour. Pamela could not possibly have known what was in Benadrylla's pockets, or what it would mean, but as she let out a long fart that shivered her tail and closed her eyes in bliss, it looked very much as though she were enjoying her revenge.

'Be assured: that wicked pair will face justice,' Stapleford Pinch announced loudly, and then whispered to Finnick, 'We can't open the railway after all that. What do I have to sign to cancel it?'

Finnick swallowed hard. 'I don't know, sir. The thing is . . . there's no form for this.'

They faced each other in utter horror.

Chapter Thirty

Stapleford Pinch allowed himself a small sigh of relief. For a minute he'd thought he was a goner. But actually, it was all going to be OK.

The map was a fraud, but it had been officially stamped and so it was now an awkward truth that there had been an 'abandoned village' in the clearing. However, permission had been granted to remove it, too, and indeed it *had* been removed – leaving an empty clearing and a clean, consistent set of paperwork. No one had to know that anything untoward had happened. Well, except everyone at the ceremony. He hoped they would all be happy to forget the trauma.

And no one had been hypnotized by that incompetent pharmacist, who was at that moment being carted off to face DEATH to account for his actions. There would be no question of Benadrylla Crumplepatch ever getting permission to build another railway, or indeed anything else. The orphans would have to be re-registered with DEATH, of course, seeing as no one seemed to know where their adoptive father was. It was for their own good.

He felt a tug at his sleeve and peered down at a serious-looking boy. 'Ah, Cuthbert, isn't it?' he asked. 'Don't you worry, sonny, we'll have you back in an orphanage soon enough.'

Cuthbert's eyes narrowed. 'Mr Pinch,' he said, 'I must draw your attention to an inconsistency in the paperwork. According to the law, Marshmallow was an abandoned settlement. Correct, sir?'

'Indeed,' Pinch agreed impatiently. 'But then it was smashed to smithereens, legally. Now off you pop. The grown-ups have work to do.'

Cuthbert waved a paper under his nose with a flourish. 'Except, Mr Pinch, that if you check carefully, the stamp is *outside* the box on the demolition permission form. And it's smudged.' He paused for effect, relishing the moment. 'Rendering it invalid.'

Pinch took it from him, hand trembling. He called Finnick over, who had a sudden memory of Benadrylla impatiently yanking the form from under his stamp the moment he'd placed it down, before passing out. He looked at his shoes.

'Marshmallow was destroyed *illegally*,' Cuthbert added, in case Pinch was in any doubt.

Pinch gazed around at the devastated clearing. 'There has been a catastrophic administrative error!' he wailed. Silence instantly fell, as a hundred FUN officials who had thought their days couldn't possibly get any worse found that in fact they could.

'You will have to rebuild,' Cuthbert pointed out smugly. 'Just as it was.'

With horror, Pinch realized the boy was right, the irritating little squirt. 'But . . . but . . .' he spluttered. 'There is no record of what it looked like.' This was turning into a nightmare. His career would be in tatters. 'I wish you had realized that all our lives would be so much easier if you'd kept this to yourself.'

'Oh I did,' said Cuthbert. 'Just before I pointed it out.'

'Excuse me,' came a small voice at Pinch's elbow. 'I can help you.'

Herc was tugging at his other sleeve and holding up what appeared to be a child's drawing. Except somehow, impossibly, it was adorned with a FUN stamp.

'You want to know what Marshmallow looked like before it was mashed up. It looked like this.'

Pinch peered at it, trying to make sense of the scrawls. 'I don't understand.'

247

'There are labels and stuff, so you can see what everything was.'

The Head Minister for FUN's lips formed the words numbly. 'Helter Skelter . . . Sky Swing . . . Mud Bath . . . *Sweet Factory*?'

Herc nodded solemnly. 'Yes. But it can't be one of those factories that makes lots of smoke, because that's not good for people, or animals. We *are* in the woods, you know.'

Pinch cast around for help, but found none. 'I'm sorry, but this is absurd.'

Herc merely pointed at the stamp, an undeniable inky logo just inside a carefully drawn box. Next to him, Finnick began to sweat heavily.

Pinch was trembling. 'No one could have built a village like this. It's a complete fantasy.'

Even with a stamp on it, this was too much. An impossibility.

'Then explain *this*.' With a flourish, Herc produced a squashed, grey blob, rescued from the remains of his kitchen. 'This marshmallow was made in that very factory.' He stabbed a finger on the map. 'Eat it, it's the best thing ever.'

Pinch stared at the object that had been pressed into his hand as though it might poison him. 'Aren't marshmallows made almost entirely of sugar?' he asked suspiciously. 'DEATH frowns on that sort of thing.' They only got away with the sweet puddings at the feast by covering them up with plenty of cream.

'Nope. They're naturally sweet.' Herc shoved his hand back in his pocket and crossed his fingers.

Everyone was watching. The last thing Pinch wanted was to eat this small, rubbery object outside of regular mealtimes, but he needed to shut this nonsense down once and for all. He popped it in his mouth.

A feeling of bliss began to spread through his body,

starting at his tongue and sending waves of intense flavour into his brain. It was as though strawberry fireworks were going off in his head, sparks crackling along his veins all the way down to his toes.

It reminded him of how he had felt as a junior assistant starting out at FUN, when he'd been allowed to use the hole punch for the first time on his own. Except this was even better.

There was no doubt about it: the boy must be telling the truth. It was several minutes before Pinch could speak.

When he did, it came out as a croak, but the words were perfectly clear. 'Get me a team of architects. NOW!'

❧ Chapter Thirty-One ❧

At least, Pinch thought, the children's father had finally turned up.

Arfur had driven his library cart into the clearing with Bernard at full speed – approximately ten miles an hour – mud churning up under the wheels, leaning into the turn as though he were competing in a chariot race. Leaping down, he proceeded to berate his children.

'You lot take the ruddy biscuit, you do. Nick my cart, go get yourselves in a world of trouble, and don't even think to mention it to your old dad? What's that stuff between your ears? Cos it ain't no use. And you –' he pointed a finger at Ashna – 'what's this I hear about you thinking that quack in Powders 'n' Potions had hypnotized me? I can't lie, Ash, I'm offended.'

'Well, I know now that he was rubbish at it, but he must've managed it a *little* bit,' she retorted. 'Come on. You were humming that tune from his clock chime, throwing all your books on the dump . . .'

He was aghast. 'You what? I said I was *taking* them to the dump. For old Lotta Gangrene to read so I could make space for me new stock. Thanks to you, I had to walk all the way with them boxes, three ruddy trips. She gets lonely, sat out there on a pile of rubbish with nuffink to do. You should have a look through me new selection, got some good comics in there.'

'Oh.' She felt silly for a moment.

'And as for that chime, it's catchy, innit?' He began to hum it again, until her expression shut him up.

Stef cut in. 'But if he was so useless at hypnotizing people, why could nobody remember anything he'd said? And why did everyone in Sad Sack think he was so great?'

'Look . . .' Arfur sighed. 'What he does, when you go in there, he makes it all woo-woo and, I'll admit, it made me a bit uncomfortable at first. He lights that smelly stuff, and true enough, it *is* kinda relaxing. And then he starts going on and on about how ruddy marvellous he is and, I'll be honest wiv you, I dropped off. All right? I ain't proud of it, but there we go. I weren't the only one.'

Stef began to understand. 'You mean . . . Cornswallop and Maisie and Ma Yeasty and everyone else . . . they weren't hypnotized *at all*? They were—'

'Bored outta their tiny minds, yeah. And he were that

full of himself, he thought they was in a trance.'

'And when they woke up they felt refreshed . . .' Ashna added.

'. . . because they'd had a nice nap, and a cuppa tea,' finished Arfur. 'And let's face it, that's enough to make most people happy. They thought he must've done something special. Once they'd convinced themselves of that, they started to see miracles everywhere. Mangy toes that got better after a decent wash, headaches that disappeared after a bit of fresh air . . .'

'But, OK, how did he bring Betty Cornswallop back to life?' asked Stef. 'Because she's definitely alive – I saw her a few days ago. You can't explain that.'

'Easiest of all.' Arfur chuckled. 'He brought her back, all right, but not from the dead – from North Hogsford, where she'd gone off in a huff to stay with her sister.'

Stef gasped. 'But everyone thought she must've fallen off a cliff or something, when she disappeared.'

'Zackly. So Bickley, he knows right enough where she is. He gets Ralph to wish for her return, while he messes about with the tea. After that, he only has to sit on his bum and wait for her to come home. Ta-da! Miracle.'

Tig sighed. 'Wow. But taking over FUN? Becoming President? Can you imagine? I thought he was just trying to flog his fake remedies and to turn people against us

253

because he hated us. Never thought he actually had big plans.'

Cuthbert shook his head. 'I suppose you don't have to be an expert hypnotist to trick people, after all.'

'Yeah,' said Arfur. 'He's like an evil genius, but wivout the genius bit. Whatever the opposite of one of those is.'

'An evil wally,' suggested Herc.

'But a crucial witness against Benadrylla,' said Ashna. 'I realized that we could never convince anyone ourselves. So I got him to do it for us.'

Arfur had to admit they'd done all right, even without his help. After he'd extracted a promise from Ashna that she wouldn't try to make him think he was a chicken or any of that hypnotic malarkey, he was in a cheery mood. Every single one of his pigeons had turned up back in the coop that morning, he told them eagerly. 'I knew it!' he kept saying to anyone who would listen. 'They found their way home to me, just like I said. Cleverest birds in Sad Sack!' When he began planning to release the pigeons much further afield to show off their homing skills, Ashna had to tell him the truth – that Joe had rescued them and driven them home.

'I'm sorry,' she said, feeling guilty as his face fell. 'But if you take them far away, you'll probably never get them back. I'm sure they love you, but they'll just hang around wherever you put them. Some pigeons are just not cut out for homing, you know?'

He looked crushed. 'I love 'em anyways,' he insisted. 'I don't care if they don't know which way is up.'

Ashna nodded sympathetically. Neither did most people in Sad Sack, she reflected. But as they had shown by pooping all over his shop sign the pigeons had, at least, always been right about Bickley Brimstone.

❧ Chapter Twenty-Two ❧

A few weeks later

Since the aborted railway opening ceremony, the children had slept at the Palatial Hotel, all expenses paid by FUN while their new dwellings were being constructed. But they spent most of their time in the woods; as Herc pointed out, they needed to make sure it was done right. Adults were slippery creatures, gullible and weak, wrong about almost everything; they had to be supervised, or disaster would ensue.

There had been some uncomfortable moments for the orphans. They had to admit to themselves and each other that they had all been right *and* wrong, in their own ways, about different things. They just hadn't paid proper attention to each other.

This was a serious failing and had to be rectified, Cuthbert said. He adjusted their meetings so that each person had a proper time to speak, without interruption. Minutes were taken. Disagreements were put to a vote, but all parties' voices were heard and considered. Herc had only found it necessary to dump water over them once more, and that was because of an over-enthusiastically toasted marshmallow catching fire, rather than to stop a fight.

Most of all, they were grateful to Pamela, for putting the final nail in the coffin of Crumplepatch Railways. They went out together to find her favourite plants, and, with some ceremony, presented them to her in a large gold-plated vessel that had once been the Sad Sack Business Association Trophy. She  knocked it over contemptuously, scooped it up on her horns and rammed it into the nearest tree before returning to munch on her treats. The trophy remained stuck fast in the trunk and nobody could pull it out.

'I don't think the chamomile is working as much on her now,' Herc observed thoughtfully. 'She must be getting used to it. I expect she'll be back to her old self soon!'

The others were less than thrilled about this.

'It's good to be back together, just us again.' Tig sighed. 'A bit of peace, finally. Once the builders have gone, anyway.'

Nellie laughed. 'You kidding? This place'll be busy. I can't wait.' She chuckled again at Tig's uncomprehending face. 'Think about it. Got ourselves a station, don't we? What, you think them trains'll be empty?'

It was true, Tig realized, her heart fluttering. Marshmallow was firmly a destination now; they'd made sure of it, without quite meaning to. Strangers would come. Whether the orphans liked it or not.

The only real sadness was for Joe. It must have hurt to realize that his mother's actions were entirely her own and not because she was hypnotized; it meant that she really was the cruel, heartless person she always had been.

The orphans might only have a semi-detached, pretend dad around, but they did have family – each other. Nobody should have a mother like Benadrylla Crumplepatch.

It was a blisteringly hot day. Summer had peaked and the leaves of the oaks around Marshmallow were crisping, ready for autumn. The building of the station was progressing well; the train shed bustled with activity. Stef checked the water level in the steam engine while the engineer watched. 'Good job,' she told him. 'You're done

258

for the day. Better go and get cleaned up.'

He stepped out, wiping his arm across his forehead, realizing too late that it was filthy with coal-dust. Not that he cared. Finally he was getting some training. He was learning fast and loving every minute of it. He wasn't sure what he wanted to end up working on, yet – the trains, the factory, the buildings . . . maybe all of it. It would be up to him to decide.

'I hope that was water this time,' a voice called from behind him. 'Not beer.'

He turned to see a small, skinny figure approaching, looking hopeful but wary, as though unsure of his welcome.

'Joe! You're back! You're not in jail!' Stef's grin nearly split his face, but turned quickly to alarm. 'Hang on – your mum's not here, is she?'

Joe shook his head ruefully and explained: no one had noticed that the driver of the DEATH carriage that had taken them away from the ceremony was not the usual one, but a woman who turned out to be from Crumplepatch Cabbies. Once they were safely far away, the DEATH officers, along with Bickley Brimstone, had found themselves thrown out on to the road, watching the horses gallop the vehicle into the distance.

Stef was taken aback. 'So . . . she got away! She's not

been processed by DEATH at all.'

He shook his head. 'She went on the run, and took me with her. FUN have taken control over Crumplepatch Industries now, so she's got nothing. She blamed me, of course. She wanted me to help her start again and get revenge on everyone.'

'I'm so sorry, Joe.' Stef laid a hand on his shoulder. 'For everything.'

Joe stared at him. 'Are you kidding? You were right about me. I tried so hard to please Mum, but nothing I did was good enough. And then you came along . . . I was there, you know, in the tent, when she said she wished you were her son. She knew I was listening. I hated you, then. That's why I tried to make trouble for you. It's me that should be sorry. And I really am.'

Stef shrugged, embarrassed. 'You had a lot to put up with.'

Joe looked up at Stef ruefully. 'Not anymore. I ran away. I heard what was happening here and I decided . . . Well, I thought I'd come stay in Marshmallow, help build it. If it's all right with you and the others, that is,' he added, glancing around at the building work, blinking slightly at the unfinished sweet factory.

Stef found himself beaming from ear to ear. 'That would be—'

They were interrupted by the sound of an argument coming from the other side of the engine, where they found Arfur waving his arms around in protest at an unmoved Finnick.

'I am sorry,' Finnick was telling him, in the patient tones of a man who has already said it twenty times and is fully prepared to say it another twenty. 'DEATH may be asleep on the job here, but as a representative of FUN I can no longer stand by and say nothing. As the person with parental responsibility, *you* are required to stay here with them.'

'I'm begging you,' Arfur tried. 'You've met 'em. They'll drive me up the wall. I ain't living here with them, not for a million quid.'

Finnick pursed his lips. 'There is no question of such a sum. Nevertheless, the children must be supervised.'

'I'll supervise 'em from Sad Sack. That little one, he's got a right powerful pair of lungs – I can just keep an ear out.'

'I'm afraid that is not sufficient. The children must be able to contact you at any time of day or night . . .' He trailed off apologetically. Personally, he could entirely understand the man's reluctance. But rules were rules. 'The fact is, an hour's tramp through the woods is inappropriate. You cannot live so far away. You are their *parent.*'

Arfur sucked his teeth as though Finnick had insulted him with a very rude word. 'Now listen here . . .' He raised his finger to jab at Finnick and then paused, with a thoughtful expression. 'So . . . I just need to be, like, easy to get a hold of. Say, fifteen minutes.'

Finnick considered. 'Ten.'

A slow smile spread across Arfur's face. 'All righty then. You stay here. I got just the thing.'

Meanwhile, a harassed-looking architect was trying to supervise the construction of a spiral wooden slide inside the oak tree, while fending off Herc. The architect was close to tears. She'd spent a week designing a small palace-like building with a balcony and stained-glass windows, on the understanding that it was for visiting VIPs, only to discover that a goat would be living in it. But this latest request was the last straw. 'I . . . I need to train a . . . what?' she said.

'A squirrel,' Herc repeated, with more patience than the woman deserved. He pronounced it slowly. 'Train it. Actually, two, because they'll need time off.'

'But . . . why?'

It really was very unclear to Herc how these people managed to reach such senior positions. They were incredibly dense. 'To take the cushions people have slid down on back to the top of the tree, of course. The squirrels can either carry them up in their mouths, or use a rope pulley.'

'But . . . that's ridiculous. You can't—'

'Yes you can. It's been done before. It has been *well documented*, in the book I showed you.' Cuthbert had been teaching Herc a few clever-sounding phrases, and the effect they had on grown-ups was amazing. If you said you didn't know something, they looked down on you, but if you said that 'the information was not currently available' it shut them right up. Right now, everything was 'well documented'.

The woman began to appeal to her colleagues but they were all suddenly fascinated by things in other directions.

Herc sighed. 'Mr Pinch!' he called over to where the Head Minister was hovering anxiously, trying to stay away from Cuthbert in case he came up with any more problems.

Pinch hurried over.

'Tell her,' Herc said.

Pinch shifted uncomfortably. 'Very well. I would very much like another marshmallow, but I'm not allowed to have one till after my dinner.'

'Not that, silly. Tell her what she has to *do*.'

'Sir! I must protest!' said the architect. 'He wishes me to train a squirrel! How am I supposed to—'

263

Pinch held up both hands in front of him to ward off the woman's argument. Nothing could be allowed to diverge from the officially approved architecture, or delay the production of marshmallows. 'Listen, I don't care if he asks you to paint your bottom red and use it as a stop sign for the trains. You do it, or we're all out of a job. If he tells you to train a squirrel, you train a squirrel, even if you have to set up an official squirrel training school and pay monkeys with peanuts to teach in it. Is that clear?'

The woman swallowed. 'Yes, sir.'

Herc stared up at Pinch admiringly.

He hadn't thought of monkeys. Monkeys would be brilliant.

Later that afternoon, Arfur appeared back in Marshmallow with a lump under his coat which, when he found Finnick and opened it, turned out to be a large grey pigeon. He thrust it into Finnick's startled arms.

'There. Sorted.'

Finnick frowned down at the pigeon, and it blinked back up at him with its blank, black eyes. It gave him no explanation. 'I . . . I don't understand.'

'That there,' said Arfur, giving the bird an affectionate pat on the head, 'is Marvin. Son of Fevvers, rest his soul. He's gonna live here now. So I don't have to.'

Finnick held the creature's warm, fat body uncertainly.
'I fear you have misunderstood . . . a pigeon is not capable
of parenting—'

'Nah. This here is a *homing* pigeon. The very best. A
finely tuned instrument of navigation. D'you know how
fast pigeons fly, mate?' Finnick shook his head. 'Good.
Well, for you and me, it's an hour to my place in Sad Sack,

right? But for a top-of-the-range bird like this, less than five minutes in the air. Geddit? He can take messages, on his leg, like. So I'm supervising, innit?'

He slapped Finnick on the back, heartily enough that Finnick staggered forward and dropped the bird, who fluttered clumsily to the ground and began to peck at his ankles.

'Really?' Finnick asked. It wasn't exactly what he'd had in mind. 'Five minutes? And it will come straight to you?'

'Course!' Arfur shook his head in wonder. 'Where you been? This is the modern world, mate. Never mind trains. It's a new era of communications!'

Finnick watched the pigeon doubtfully for a few moments. It waddled around him, and then directed a stream of pale, mucky liquid on to his shoe.

When he looked up, Arfur was nowhere to be seen.

THE END

Acknowledgements

I had enormous fun writing this book. But there are a lot of people who made the process much easier and without whose help it wouldn't be here at all. Thanks are due to all the following.

David Tazzyman – for making me laugh so much with a few strokes of a pencil, bringing the world of St Halibut's to life.

Kate Shaw, for having my back, and for emailing me pictures of your beagle puppy, Nell, in my hours of need.

Cate Augustin and Lucy Pearse, the best editors I could wish for – I am so grateful for your sharp eyes, editorial genius, and accidental-euphemism-spotting talents.

The whole Macmillan team, including Samantha Smith, Sarah Clarke, Rachel Graves, Laura Carter, Tracey Ridgewell, Rachel Vale, Sabina Maharjan, Nick de Somogyi, Charlie Selvaggi-Castelletti.

I will always be grateful to Michael Rosen – champion

of writers and readers all over the world – for kick-starting my publishing journey in 2012 by picking me as a short-story competition winner.

Rebecca Instone at Buttercups Goat Sanctuary, for answering my questions and introducing me to some of Pamela's less headbutty cousins. Any remaining goat-related inaccuracies are all my own fault.

Tiggy and Ashna – look, I know I said I'd give your names back last time, but they're kind of busy in St Halibut's at the moment. Sorry, and thanks.

The Swaggers, for niche GIFs and friendship.

Mad, Nick, Evie and Olivia for support and for taking me running even though I am much slower than all of you.

Rob, Fraser, and Cameron for inspiration, feedback, encouragement, interruption, understanding, coffee-bringing, and love.

Finally, the real Pamela, for giving me all those memories that still occasionally cause me to wake up in the middle of the night, shouting 'Close the gate!' in panic. If by some miracle you're still alive, please don't try to find me.

About the Author and Illustrator

Sophie Wills grew up in Chelmsford, Essex. She failed the 11+, had a weekend job at a boarding kennels where she suffered workplace bullying from a goat and nurtured a dream to have a career she could do in her pyjamas.

She entered Mumsnet's first Bedtime Story competition in 2012 and Michael Rosen picked out as a winner her story about a pig-riding sheriff.

She lives on the edge of south-east London with her family.

David Tazzyman is an internationally acclaimed, award-winning and million-copy bestselling illustrator. He worked as a commercial illustrator before falling into children's publishing in 2006, illustrating Andy Stanton's Mr Gum series which went on to win numerous awards, including the first Roald Dahl Funny Prize in 2008. Now David mainly illustrates children's picture and fiction books and lives in Leicestershire with his partner and three children.